Meet me at the

Bus Stop

Arrowsmith High Series

MJ Ray

Meet Me at the Bus Stop

(Arrowsmith High #1)

Published by MJ Ray

November 2020

I dedicate this book to my daughter, Isabelle, who has inherited my love of reading and inspired me to write this book.

Prologue

Rosie

"Mum, I need to leave now, or I'll miss the bus!" *How bad would that be on the first day?*

"Okay . . . Okay, so you've got your salad, right? And your fruit and water?"

I roll my eyes; God forbid that I would forget my salad and need to eat something that actually tastes good. It's the first of many times today that she will mention my weight. As I'm being reminded by her daily, I need to watch what I eat. Curves are very bad in her eyes.

"Yeah, I've got them. I'll still be hungry after I've eaten, but I've got them."

"You know by now: no pain, no gain. Go on, have a great first day."

As I step out into the bleak, rainy day, nerves seriously start to kick in. Who moves schools in their last year? Me, that's who. Let's hope I've done the right thing . . . nothing can be as awful as my previous school. The only way is up.

Great . . . nearing the bus stop, I take in the people already standing there. Everyone looks so relaxed while I feel so intimidated. Why does everyone seem so together and good looking? I *hate* being the new girl.

I check my uniform is as good as it can be and straighten up my tie; at least there's only one more year of wearing this thing. I've seen worse uniforms though – something to be thankful for. The navy blue and yellow checked skirt teamed with the navy jumper are pretty tasteful. Any school uniform would look ridiculous on me, though; my size 16 frame with larger-than-average boobs makes it seem like I'm trying to force an adult's body into a child's outfit.

There are six others from my school there. The two boys that are undoubtedly twins who aren't in uniform - they must be in the sixth form. There is a tall, slim, glamorous girl with gorgeous, straight, long blonde hair; she looks like she should be in a magazine. A beautiful girl with red, curly hair piled up in a messy bun, I like the look of her; she looks approachable. There is a scary-looking girl with jet black hair that is finding her feet rather interesting, I can't see her face. Lastly, there is a big guy that's kind of attractive, tall and broad with longish hair. None of them have seen me yet. I'm just an outsider looking in. I hate this feeling, the feeling that I'm going to throw up or need the toilet. I hate nerves, and I'm packed full of them today.

The girl with red hair smiles at me as I near the group. She looks natural with no make-up, my kind of girl. We're not supposed to wear make-up at school, but there are always girls that bend the rules. Some girls perfect the art of taking hours to put on makeup in the morning so that it looks like they're not wearing any. The smiling girl is beautiful; she has freckles and green eyes. Relief washes over me that she is friendly. It looks like she's about to speak to me when a small minibus comes around the corner; I guess this is our ride. It looks decrepit, and I have my doubts that it will make it to school. Beggars can't be choosers. Mum and Dad both work, and Russ has college on the other side of the village. If I thought it was any use, I would have begged them to take me instead.

"Here it is, our good, old, trusty steed. One day, they might give us an upgrade," one of the boys says, the one with longish brown hair. He's laughing and shaking his head. "I can't believe they're getting another year out of it! This is our punishment for living out of the way of the bus route."

I hate to say it, but I think he might be right!

The bus pulls up to us. Yup, it's ours. It's just my luck that I live so far out from Arrowsmith High that I have to get on this special minibus. Someone left school at the end of last year, which meant there was a spot for little old me; it's only an eight-seater.

So, these are the guys that I'll be sharing the bus with all year. *Please be nice.*

The double doors creak open, and a man with grey hair shouts, "Good morning, young people!" He's grinning and looking like the happiest guy on earth. *He knows we're going to school, right?*

We all bundle on the bus, the day so wet and miserable that I'm glad to get undercover. I try not to look at anyone as I climb on. When I look for somewhere to sit, the friendly girl smiles and waves at me; she motions for me to go and sit with her. Gratefully, I make my way toward her. That's when it happens, the most mortifying thing that could happen on your first day at school when you don't know anyone.

I mentioned it was raining, right?

My shoe loses its footing on the wet floor of the bus, and before I can grab anything, I slide along the bus as though I'm water skiing, practically doing the splits. Quite a performance, really.

I'm a second away from hitting the deck in full force when a pair of arms close around me to steady me. "Whoa there! You been drinking already? School hasn't even started."

I look up and suddenly feel like I *have* been drinking. The most beautiful blue eyes are staring down at me with a twinkle in them.

"I . . . Where did you come from?"

"I was late, just caught Tony here before he sets off and—lucky for you—just caught you before *you* set off." He laughs.

I hear someone mutter, "Late as usual. First day as well."

He ignores whoever it is. "If I let you go, will you stay upright?" Beautiful Eyes Guy raises his eyebrows. He is so good looking and tall. He's in uniform, so he's got to be in the last year. He looks too old to be wearing it. Still . . . I imagine he would look good in anything.

I nod numbly, and he lets me go. I try to find my voice, but it has left the building. Or... the minibus. Releasing me, he gives me a nod and a small smile. He swings in next to one of the twins, giving him a chin lift, the universal hello for guys.

I sit down in my seat, trying to process what just happened. I want the ground to swallow me up. That . . . Well, it was my worst nightmare. If I could somehow get invisibility powers around about now, that would be great.

I sit next to the nice girl. "Are you okay?" she leans in and says quietly.

I give her a sorry excuse for a smile. "No . . . I mean physically, yes, but just absolutely mortified."

She shrugs. "Aw . . . Don't worry. I'm sure you'll laugh at it later."

Will I, though?

She carries on. "At least it's just us eight and not a full schoolyard; look on the bright side."

She's right; that would have been even worse. "Yeah, you're right. Not the way I wanted to make an entrance though. I'm more of a 'keep quiet and hope nobody notices me' kind of girl." I smile at her. "I'm Rosie."

"Riley," she answers.

The bus driver speaks, addressing my knight in shining armour. "You nearly missed this then, laddie. Where would you be then? First day of school and in trouble."

Knight Guy—yes, I'm calling him Knight Guy now—shrugs. "Nothing new there." He slumps down in his seat, putting his earphones on.

The bus driver looks at the rest of us. "Right. I see a lot of familiar faces, and I'm sure you all missed me desperately. It is good to be back. But there *is* a face I don't know." He looks at me, "Nearly came a cropper there, lass. Sorry. This floor can get a bit slippery when it's wet."

Okay, mortification continuing. I don't want anyone to talk about it ever!

He continues. "I'm Tony." He smiles kindly; I know he doesn't mean to embarrass me.

Riley motions toward me. "This here is Rosie."

He gives me a big, genuine smile. "Welcome, Rosie. Pleased to meet you. They're not a bad bunch, these guys, when you get to know them."

"Thanks, Tony. Nice to meet you, too," I say in a quiet voice and then put my head down, my cheeks still on fire because I've embarrassed myself so much in the first five minutes and hate that all attention is on me. I suppose I had better get used to it today. I'll hopefully get all my firsts over with this week. Then, I should just be able to blend in and get on with surviving school.

Tony, seemingly satisfied that we all have our seatbelts on, sets off on my first journey to Arrowsmith High.

Riley leans into me. "You'll get used to us. We all know each other pretty well because there are so few of us, and we do this twice a day. But not many of us hang out at school together. So, you're new? I've never seen you around school."

I nod. "Yeah, I'm new. I used to go to Sablewood Academy but transferred here over the summer."

"Wow. Sablewood Academy? How posh!"

I roll my eyes. "Yeah . . . It was horrible; I hated it."

"Only the gifted and rich go there, right? So, which are you?"

I like her openness. At least she's saying what she's thinking rather than gossiping behind my back. I already like this school better.

I answer her. "Well, I suppose a bit of both. I was on a half scholarship . . . I guess I'm pretty good at maths."

She nods. "Cool! A genius. I know where to come if I need help. Are you in year 11?"

"Yeah. A nightmare, I know, starting in the last year but had to be done."

Please don't ask why I've moved schools.

Luckily, she doesn't pry. "You look older than sixteen."

I nod. "Yeah, not the first time I've heard that." I look down at my boobs and point to them. "These don't help."

She laughs, "I bet not. I'm still waitin' for mine."

Am I really talking to her about my boobs in the first five minutes of meeting her?

"I wish I was still waiting for mine." That is no joke; I do. I hate that they're so big for my age. They come with unwanted attention.

She seems nice, and she's been open with me. So, I decide to be open with her. "Anyway . . . Thanks for letting me sit next to you. I'm pretty terrified, to be honest."

"Aw, it's okay. I know it must be horrible being new, especially starting in the last year. You can hang out with me at school; I'm in year eleven, too. I'll introduce you to my friends, you know, if you want to?"

I could cry with relief. "Thank you so much. That would be great."

"No problem." She calls out to the glamorous girl, "Harper, meet Rosie. She's in our year."

Harper looks over and smiles. Wow, she's pretty, but when she smiles, it transforms her whole face. She's gorgeous. "Welcome, Rosie; good to meet you."

I swallow nervously, not liking that her attention is on me. I don't have good experiences with girls like Harper. That's the reason I'm here right now, in fact. "Nice to meet you."

Riley carries on. "Harper hangs with the rich and the beautiful, don't you hun?"

Harper rolls her eyes. "Whatevs, Riles. You're just jealous." The words are mean, but the tone is not. They're joking around, comfortable with each other.

Riley carries on to me in a low voice. "She's really good friends with the twins, Edward and Cooper. Edward is her best friend. The three of them practically grew up together, so they're always together. The twins are in sixth form, though."

I turn to her and whisper, "Who's the guy who grabbed me?"

She looks at me knowingly. "Don't tell me you've fallen for his charms already? Well, quite literally, I suppose." She laughs.

Oh, God... Did I make it look obvious that I thought he was hot? "No . . . No . . . I just wondered who he was."

"That's Liam. The year six heartthrob. Most girls want to try him out, and most already have, to be honest. Not me, though. He barely knows my name."

She glances over at him. "I like him . . . Most of the girls do, but he can have his pick." She looks at me sadly, "It's okay . . . I just love him from afar."

Sympathy washes over me. It must be hard. The last guy I would want to fall for is the one that everyone wants. "There's always one of those guys in every school, I guess." I can't say I'm surprised though; he has a demeanour about him that screams bad boy. There aren't many guys around that look like he does; it makes sense that he'd get lots of attention.

She gives me a sad smile. "Yeah, I guess there is. I don't have time for boys anyway. I train sixteen hours a week."

My eyes widen. "*What?* What do you do?"

"Gymnastics. All my spare time is spent at the gym. My coach says that if I put the work in, I will make the Olympics in 2024, but I've got a long way to go yet. I've won lots of comps, but I want a gold medal . . . God, do I want a gold medal." She gets a dreamy look in her eyes.

"Wow! That is amazing. Where do you get your energy from? And, how do you fit it all in with school and other stuff?"

"I have to make the time. If you want something badly enough, you've got to make it happen, right? I'm going to make it, and I am going to get that gold medal. It will be worth the hard work when I'm standing up on that podium."

I admire her determination. I don't think I've ever wanted something so badly that I won't take no for an answer. She is so strong - I could learn a thing or two from her.

One of the twins leans over to us. "Got any gum, Riles?" He looks nice. He has kind eyes and a genuine smile.

She fiddles in her bag and hands him one.

He takes it and looks at me. "Hey, I'm Edward. My miserable excuse for a brother here is Cooper." Cooper looks at his brother with a scowl then turns to me and gives me a chin lift, too cool to speak. I get it. I didn't know twins could look identical but seem so different. Edward seems friendly and approachable. Cooper, on the other hand, looks scary, as though he is thinking evil thoughts about you. He's not as happy as his brother for whatever reason.

The larger guy with the longish hair speaks up. "I'm Charlie. I'm in year ten. I'm the baby of the bus."

That surprises me because he is so tall and is carrying a little weight; it makes him look older. He might be the youngest, but he is very handsome.

"Nice to meet you." I try not to blush. I'm not good at talking to boys, especially not attractive ones, and this bus is full of them.

That leaves the scary-looking girl. She already has her earphones in and doesn't look up.

Charlie asks, "You always this quiet?"

Huh... I never used to be. I used to be fun, but I barely remember that person, the person I was before Holly and her gang. Three years of relentless bullying and turning the whole school against me. I've forgotten who I was before all that started. I give myself a mental shake. I don't need to be that person anymore; I'm at a school where no one knows me, and I can be whoever I want, whatever personality I want. The trouble is that I have no idea who I am anymore.

"I'm sorry. Until I get to know someone, I may come across a little shy but give me time." I muster up confidence from somewhere.

So, a year of travelling with these people. Twins, an athlete, an "it" girl, a funny guy, a quiet and scary girl, and the hottest guy I have ever seen. Riley is being friendly with me. It could be worse, a hell of a lot worse.

Come on, Rosie. Let's see if you can make this year better than the last few .

. .

Chapter One

Rosie

Two months later . . .

"Seriously, you should have seen it, Rosie. He stood, threw his book across the room, and stormed out. The whole class was silent," Riley says to me, filling me in on Liam's antics from today. He is always in trouble for one reason or another. It's like he has a death wish when he gets to school.

I shake my head. *Liam, why?* "He must be having a hard time somehow; maybe something is going on at home. He's great on the bus. I don't get it; he always seems happy, but everyone you speak to says he's trouble. Why does he always cause so much trouble in class? There must be a reason."

She sighs. "I don't know, but I do worry about him. It is possible that he's just an idiot, though."

I shake my head. "Maybe, but I don't think so, and I know you don't either. Something is up with him." I know it's not our place to find out what, but I can't help feeling that all this trouble is a cry for help. Who knows? Maybe he likes the attention. He doesn't come across that way on the bus, though. His personality seems chilled and easy to get on with; it's like he flips a switch when entering the school gates.

I have a problem. My name is Rosie, and I'm a Liamaholic.

It was only a matter of time, I guess. I've joined in with the rest of the females in school and gone and gotten a crush on the most unattainable guy, one that is *so* the complete opposite from me that it's not even funny. To make matters worse, Liam is Riley's favourite subject; she loves to talk about him, and there is always lots to say on the subject as he's constantly getting into trouble. She has it bad for him. I feel for her because he doesn't look her way, but he doesn't look my way, either. There's no way that I can tell her that I like him, too; she'll be upset. It's not like anything could happen with him and me, but still, she wouldn't like it. Why am I crushing on him anyway? I would never go for someone like him if I were keeping my head. He's not someone I would ever want to be with. He's loud, brash, rebellious, arrogant, and likes being the centre of attention.

Why is he always in trouble, though? It's like he's mad at the world. It upsets me that everyone thinks so poorly of him all the time when I know he can be a nice guy.

Riley shrugs. "I guess . . . Who knows? He is extremely nice to all the pretty girls but never to me."

"Or me. Well, apart from when he caught me on the first day. That was nice of him, even if it was embarrassing."

"Yeah . . . That was awesome. You had his arms around you." She sighs. "He's just *so* pretty."

"Yeah, but the guy has issues, obviously. You wouldn't want to go there. He's trouble, plain and simple."

I know . . . I'm being a hypocrite, but he would never in a million years look my way. I just like looking at him from afar. It's fun to daydream about him. It's not like anything could happen in real life."

"I guess you're right, but I can't help thinking that I'm the one that he would change his ways for, you know?"

"Yeah, but *every* girl thinks that about a bad boy."

"I'm obviously living in a dream world."

"You deserve someone who knows how special you are. You will get that; I'm sure of it."

She rolls her eyes. "You're my friend; you have to say that. What about you, anyway? Anyone you have your eye on?"

I swallow and look away. "Don't be silly. No one would be interested in me."

She frowns. "Rosie, it makes me mad when you say things like that. When you look in the mirror, you don't see what everyone else sees. What can I do to get you to think more of yourself? You're seriously gorgeous, honestly. Those big blue eyes and your lovely brown thick hair, which most girls would die for by the way... But it's those lips. Surely, you've noticed that when boys talk to you, they watch your mouth move? Those full lips draw them in like a moth to a flame. Not to mention, as much as you try to hide them, you're rather endowed in the bosom department."

I flush bright red. "You're sweet, but I can't see any moths hanging around. You're my friend, so you only see the good stuff. But what about this?" I grab my stomach and my thighs; there is way more than a handful.

"That is your mum talking, and you know it. I know you're conscious of your weight, but I wish you could see from my point of view how crazy that is. You have serious curves girl, a body any girl would want. Don't think I haven't noticed how you fix your uniform as best you can so as not to show off what you think are your problem areas when, in fact, they're assets."

I look down to the floor, I confided in her a few weeks ago about my mum and what she's like with the pressure for me to lose weight, to eat healthily—to barely eat anything really.

"You are lovely but I can't help it. There's only so many times you can be told something before it's drummed into you. We can't all look like you, you know."

"I look like a boy: no hips, no boobs. I know it's because of all the gymnastics I do. If I do want to make it to the Olympics, I have to not care about this stuff. What are we like? Both wishing we looked more like each other. Plus, all this training is taking its toll on my body. Who knows how I'm going to suffer for it later in life? But for now, if I didn't have long hair, everyone would think I was a boy."

"No one in a million years could *ever* mistake you for a boy." She talks about me selling myself short; she is so pretty.

She shrugs. "Thanks . . . I don't believe you, but thanks."

I throw my arm around her and guide her to the dining hall. "Come on. Let's go and find something to eat that your coach and my mum would faint over if they saw us eating."

It's been two months since I first got on that bus. I'm good now. This school is a lot better than my other, that's for sure. I sit next to Riley every day; we save each other a seat. Harper sits by us, too. She and the twins are close friends, but she sits with us, usually on the way home. Edward has basketball practise a few nights a week. Harper is a lot nicer than I thought she would be.

As we reach the hall, I see the goodness that is Liam running towards us. Why does my heartbeat start playing a merry tune every time I see him? Sometimes, I feel like other people can actually hear it. They can't, of course, but that's how loud it feels sometimes. He is *so* attractive; he knows it, though. He's spotted with a different girl every week. He's probably making sure they all get their turn... How sweet! Sometimes, he talks to us on the bus, but mostly, he puts his earphones in and ignores us. For a few nights a week, he doesn't even get the bus home. He has basketball training. I know that, some nights, he's with the team. The other nights, I think he's probably in detention.

He's definitely coming over to talk to us right now. I fight the urge to look behind us to see if he's going to someone else. Nope, it's us. He never usually speaks to us in the school day. He'll nod if he passes me in the corridor, but that's about it.

He reaches us and looks at me. "Rosie, I've been looking for you."

Okay, have I fallen asleep? This can't be happening. I love how he says my name; his northern accent is stronger than mine.

He continues, "Is what I've heard about you true?"

What? What could he have heard about me? No one knows about my feelings for him. My stomach sinks. Is someone saying something mean about me?

I clear my throat. "Depends . . . What have you heard?"

"That you're some sort of genius or something?" He raises his eyebrows.

I flush with embarrassment. At Sablewood Academy, it wasn't that unusual to excel at something. It was pretty much scholarship led and was hard to get into; the kids that went there were either rich or extremely good at something. Here, things are a little different. The teachers have made a big deal about my maths abilities; I didn't know it would be such a big thing.

"Er, I'm okay, I guess?"

He frowns. Is it wrong that I love his eyebrows?

Stop ogling, Rosie.

"I heard you were, like, a genius at maths."

I shrug. What does he want me to say? If I say I'm good, I'm showing off.

Riley chimes in, "She *is* a genius at maths; she just doesn't want to say."

I shoot her a dirty look.

He looks relieved. "I need your help. I mean *really* need your help. I have to hand in my maths homework this afternoon. If I don't, they won't let me play in the game on Friday, but there's no way I can do it during lunch break without help. Please will you help me?"

I'm speechless. He wants me to sit next to him, right next to him, and help him with maths? Would my brain even work properly sitting so close to him?

Riley speaks. "You didn't do your homework? That doesn't sound like you." Her voice is all flirty and girly. I have to bite back a laugh.

He rolls his eyes. "Shut up. I'm not asking you, am I?"

He looks back at me and raises his eyebrows, those stunning blue eyes staring at me, waiting for a response. I daren't look at Riley. I can feel her watching me, waiting for my answer. What should I do? Will she be mad if I say yes? He doesn't look at me that way at all, so she has nothing to worry about. Plus, it would be nice, getting to sit with him, talk to him. It would give me something to replay all night in my head when I get home.

I look up at him. Wow, he's tall; my eyes are only at his shoulders. Those eyes . . . "Yeah, sure . . . I guess I can help you."

He looks so relieved and puts a hand on my arm. "Thank you. I owe you one."

I point to the dining hall. "I'll get some lunch and meet you in the library in five minutes, okay?"

"God, thanks. See you in five," he says, grinning and running off.

I speak up before Riley gets a chance to. "Don't fall out with me . . . please? I couldn't say no; he needed my help. He looked so desperate."

"I don't mind. You will tell me any info that he gives you, right?"

My heart sinks. No, I don't want to do that. I nod and smile but don't say anything.
*****

I turn up at the library and look around. He's sat at one of the tables, drumming his fingers on the table while frowning at his book. My heart goes out to him. He isn't in my group for maths, so I don't know what level he's at. But he looks puzzled; that's for sure.

I walk up behind him, feeling nervous. "Hey . . . I'm here. Ready to get started?"

"Thank you for doing this . . . Yeah, sit down. This is what I have to do." He slides his book towards me.

I sit down next to him. I'm sitting so close that I can smell him. I mean, I don't lean in to sniff him—as tempting as that might be—but his aroma is wafting up to my nostrils. It's a mix of aftershave, fabric conditioner, and an earthy smell I can't fathom. But all together, the combination is delightful. His thigh is close to mine; it's nearly touching.

Concentrate, Rosie.

I look at the work. I can do it with my eyes closed. I don't even need to think about maths; I just get it, almost like a talent or something. I have no idea where it came from, but there hasn't been a problem I couldn't solve yet. The teachers here are impressed; I can tell. I can't help it. I understand whatever they give me. I would rather my talent be in other areas, if I'm honest: confidence, popularity maybe. But I'll take it; at least there's something I can do.

15

I explain to him what he needs to do and jot down a way for him to work it out. He gets it quickly. I'm sure not to be condescending. I find it easy, but that would be so insulting and rude. It turns out that he is rather good at maths; he just needed it explained to him once more.

Ten minutes later, he's all finished. He throws his pen down on the table and leans back in his chair. He has the sleeves of his shirt rolled up, and his tie is loosened. He looks so scruffy in his uniform, but *damn...* He makes scruffy look good. He looks over at me with those piercing blue eyes; they remind me of one of those lagoons that you see on the internet, a meme saying, *"Don't you want to be swimming here right now?"* Well, I am right now, swimming in those gorgeous eyes and drowning fast.

"I can't thank you enough."

"It's okay; no problem." I smile.

He points to his book. "So, you find this stuff easy, huh?"

I shrug. "Yeah, I guess. We all have our special talents, right?"

He chuckles. "I guess so."

"What's yours?" I ask him. *Apart from making all women forget their name, that is.*

He gives me a wink. "Now, that would be telling."

Jeez! He winked at me. How hot is it when an attractive guy winks? I get goosebumps. I blush. Why did the human body need to have the ability to blush? It is so embarrassing. Is he flirting with me? I guess he flirts with all the girls, and I bet he even flirts with the staff.

"You embarrass easily, don't you?"

Ah, he picked up on that then. "Don't . . . I hate it. I swear I blush for everything. It's the worst."

He looks at me thoughtfully. "I don't know; it's not the *worst* thing."

His eyes hold mine for a little longer than they should, silence filling the air between us. He glances down at my mouth and then back up to my eyes. *What is he thinking?*

He finally speaks, breaking the tension. "I suddenly have an amazing idea, a way to say thank you."

Kiss me... That would be thank you enough.

That's what I want to say, but of course, I don't. "What is that?"

"Connor is holding a party Saturday night."

I've only been here at Arrowsmith a short while, but even I know that Connor's parties are famous. They're wild, loud, and someone usually ends up getting arrested. Well, *maybe* I'm over-exaggerating, but they're definitely wild. Gossip on a Monday morning from these parties is always something to look forward to. Harper usually fills us in.

"Yeah . . .?"

"Well, you could go with me."

I lean back in my chair shocked that, number one, that he would want to take me—even if it is out of some sort of gratitude—but two, that he thinks I would like to go. Riley would kill me.

"Um, thanks but no thanks."

He raises his eyebrows. "Wow. That's something I don't hear very often."

I give a short laugh. "I bet," I mutter, but he hears.

He chuckles. "I think it would do you good; you're not the best mixer, but you might get to know a few people, make some friends. I think you literally have one at the moment: Riley. Surely you want more than one friend?"

How the hell does he know how many friends I have? "Again, no thanks . . . I don't like people."

"Why not?"

Like I'm going to tell him. "I just don't."

He shrugs. "I think you should make an effort."

I want to tell him to get lost, I really do, but then there is that voice again, the one that's telling me that not all girls are mean, that I'm in a new school where no one knows what happened at my last school, and that I should push myself. The trouble is that actually going somewhere with Liam, other than to and from school, fills me with both dread and excitement in equal measures.

"But you mean to go with you?"

"Yeah. What's so weird about that?"

"Won't people wonder why you're with me?"

He frowns. "What the hell? Why would anyone wonder that? What's it got to do with anyone else? I'm helping you out, right?"

Of course. That's just what it is. I stupidly was building it up inside my head that it was something more than that, that maybe he wanted to go *with* me.

Should I do it? I promised myself I would try to fit in, try and find out who I am again. His suggestion is a perfect opportunity, and anyway, if I hate it, I could leave. I'm sure Riley would be okay with it; it means he won't be with any other girls.

"Okay. Yes, I'll come . . . Thank you." I feel sick.

I watch in awe as his whole face warms as a grin spreads over his face. "Great! I'll show you how to have a good time."

I have to leave to go and have a nervous breakdown somewhere in the caretaker's cupboard where I can hyperventilate in peace. Did I just agree to go on a date with Liam, the hottest and most sought-after guy in school?

Chapter Two

Rosie

"Please, please, *please* pick up." I can hear ringing, and then, it goes to voice mail. *No!* What will I do now? I need help. If I don't get help getting ready for this date, I'm going to lose it and cancel. I should know that Riley is busy; she'll be training and have her phone in her locker at the gym. Who else can help me? I fleetingly think of Harper. Could I phone Harper? I did hang with her and Riley last weekend. She came shopping with us, and yes, she is very into makeup, clothes, selfies, Instagram, and Tik Tok, but isn't that exactly what I need right now? Advice on hair and clothes? I could ask her to help; she doesn't need to know about my crush on Liam.

I dial her number, and she answers on the first ring.

"Rosie! How's it going? What are you up to?"

"I'm getting ready for Connor's party tonight. I'm kind of hoping that you might not be busy and can help me out."

She's silent for a moment. "You're going to Connor's party?"

"Yeah . . . Why?"

"No reason; I just didn't think it would be your kind of thing, but it's great you're going. I'm going, too. We can go together . . . Wait, you wouldn't go on your own. Who are you going with?"

"Um . . . Maybe Liam?"

"Is that a question or an answer?"

I give a nervous laugh. "An answer, I guess."

"You-you're going to Connor's party with Liam?" she asks.

My heart sinks. Her reaction is what everyone's reaction will be. Why did I think that one high school would be any different from another? People are just mean. End of story.

"Yeah, I helped him with some work, so he said he would pay me back by taking me to Connor's party. I'm hanging out with him just to see what the party scene is like; it's not like it's a date or anything. I know Liam wouldn't go out with me."

"Why would he not?"

"Well, you know . . . How I look?"

"What are you talking about?"

I don't want to explain how I feel about my appearance. "Nothing . . . Never mind. But the thing is, Harper, I'm getting so close to cancelling. I am stressing about what to wear. I can go and buy something, but I don't have long. And, honestly . . . I'm terrified about going."

"You live on Richmond Drive, right?"

I nod, even though she can't see me. "Yeah, number seven."

"My dad is in; I'll ask him to drop me at yours, and we can get the V-line into Manchester. We will get you kitted out."

I sag with relief. "Thank you so much, Harper. I owe you one."

"You're kidding, right? Shopping is, like, my favourite pass-time, and I get to be your personal shopper. I'm excited!"

"I'm glad one of us is," I say, laughing.

We hang up, and I go to get ready straight away.
*****

Okay. I will *not* look out of the window again. I will *not* look out of the window again. It's ten to eight; he isn't even due yet, for goodness sake. He is going to call at my house on the way to Connor's house. Connor, as it happens, only lives around the corner.

My heart sinks as my mum walks into the room. "You look lovely, sweetheart. I see all that healthy eating is paying off."

Shut up, Mum. It's comments like that that make me feel the way I do about myself. She is obsessed about losing weight, about dieting . . . She thinks that I should be the same. She is projecting all her issues onto me as if I don't have enough. The trouble is that the worse I feel about myself, about my weight, the more I seem to eat; it's a vicious cycle. Having a crush on Liam is having a positive effect on my weight, though; my appetite has diminished a little since my stomach keeps flipping every time I see him.

He. Is. Coming. To. My. House.

I can't believe that in 10 minutes, he will be walking down my path.

Fear suddenly grips me. What if it was a joke? Surely, he wouldn't be that mean. What if it was some sort of bet? It wouldn't be the first time a guy has been cruel to me. *Right. Rosie, pull yourself together. It's not like that. You're not there; you're here. They're different people.*

"Yeah. Thanks, Mum." I say it sarcastically, but she doesn't even notice.

"Where did you get that top, love?" I can feel her eyes on me. I wish she'd just leave me alone.

I look down. I do love my new top; it's purple and fitted with puff sleeves. I've teamed it with some faded, fitted jeans that I already had. Today, Harper talked me into buying some boots from River Island that just totally set off the look. I'm so grateful for her today. What if I'd have turned up in a party dress or something? I shudder; it doesn't bear thinking about.

"It's from Top Shop."

She looks surprised. "Oh, do they do plus sizes there?"

It's a wonder I actually have the confidence to leave the house. Believe it or not, she doesn't mean to be insulting; she's just obsessed with body shape and size and doesn't think anything about commenting on my size. She has no filter. It appears that she has forgotten what it is like to be a teenager or a human being even. She knows I'm going on a date, and she doesn't think for one second that her comments could make me feel bad about myself at a time when it's important to feel nice.

"No, Mum. It's a size 14."

Her eyes widen. "Oh, right, love. Well, you look lovely."

Do you see what I have to live with?

I was severely bullied at school for three years, and this is the mother I had to come home to. If it weren't for my dad and brother, I would have gone insane. My brother, Russ, is in his last year of college, so I don't see much of him. But he was around when he could be, when I needed him the most. He doesn't say much, but he's that kind of person, the kind that doesn't need to. I knew I had him there with me every step of the way. I don't think he'll ever realise what he did for me when I was at my lowest.

I see Russ coming down the stairs; he must have caught what Mum said.

"Leave her alone, Mum." He rolls his eyes at me. He's always telling me to ignore her, that I'm fine just the way I am. Just doing his big brother duties, I suppose.

"What, Russell? I'm telling her she looks lovely."

Russ comes over, kisses me on the cheek, and mutters to me, "Yeah, in that unusual way of hers."

I give him a small smile.

"So, where are you off to tonight all dressed up?"

I'm just about to answer when there's a knock at the door. My stomach flips, but before I can answer, Russ dives at the front door. Russ is tall and well built. He does a lot of Jujitsu, something that he started at an early age, and now he's a black belt. I can imagine he's quite intimidating to some. My dog, Sky, starts to bark. She's a rescue German Shepherd that we swear must be crossed with a Great Dane or something equally as big, because she is enormous. I guess we will never know. She can be intimidating, too. It can be hard for new people to accept how timid she is. She is so friendly, but she looks scary on the outside. But my brother *definitely* looks scary on the outside.

I usher Sky into the kitchen.

"Hey, I'm here for Rosie." I hear Liam's deep voice.

"Oh, are you?" Russ asks.

Russ will make him squirm on purpose, so I rush over and shoulder him out of the way.

I look at Liam. "Hey, sorry. Don't take any notice of my brother."

Russ shouts out, "Yeah, dude. Take notice. Take *a lot* of notice." He grins, walking away and gives me a wink.

I roll my eyes and turn back to Liam who's looking at me, startled.

I give him a nervous smile. "Don't take any notice. I'm ready. I'll just grab my jacket and bag. Do you want to come in?"

He shakes his head. "No; I think I'll stay here."

I give a little laugh and grab my things. I can't help noticing how good he looks. He has on dark jeans, trainers, and a black jacket. He doesn't even need to try, and he looks good. My mouth is dry. People are going to see us walking down the street in a minute and think that he's with me. I love that.

I close the door behind me and walk to him, standing at the bottom of the path. "Sorry about that. My brother was just trying to make you squirm. I never got a chance to tell him that this wasn't a date. He just presumed, and he likes to have his fun."

Liam shakes his head. "It's no problem. Maybe fill him in when you get home, though, yeah?"

My heart sinks. I mean, I knew this wasn't a date, but it's not nice hearing it confirmed. "I will."

Silence stretches between us as we walk. The night is so cold that our warm breath is visible against the cold air.

"You look . . . You look nice, Rosie."

I blush again; hopefully, he can't see in the dark. "Thank you. I didn't know what to wear to a house party, so Harper helped me. She's coming tonight."

"Well, you're perfect . . . I mean . . . What you're wearing is perfect. Your hair is so long. I've only ever seen it tied up at school."

I shrug. "I'm a no-fuss kind of girl. Hair up, no make-up. I guess that's when I'm at my most comfortable."

He nods as we approach Connor's house. "You should do what makes you happy; if you don't like makeup and getting dressed up, you didn't have to tonight."

"Oh, no. I needed my armour for tonight."

He raises his eyebrows. "Why? We going into battle?"

"If the high school parties I went to at my old school are anything to go by, then yes."

"You weren't happy at your old school?"

I shake my head. "No . . . I wasn't."

He looks at me but doesn't say anything as we get to the front door.

I'm unsure about what to do once we're in there. Liam knows everyone here, and all eyes are on me. They're wondering what I'm doing here, why I'm here with him.

I feel Liam's hand touch mine, and I look up at him. Those blue eyes, with the crinkles at the corners as he smiles at me, send heat rushing all through my body. "Come on. Let's go into the kitchen, and I'll get you a drink." He's noticed that everyone is looking at me and knew it must have been making me feel uncomfortable. Is it possible to fall in love with someone there and then on the spot? So relieved I've got something to do, I step forward. I feel his hand in the small of my back, guiding me through the people milling around. The heat of his hand burns through my top as though it's on my bare skin. His proprietary touch is making me feel looked after. I need to keep a clear head. *This is not a date.* I'm just going to revel in the fact that I'm here with him, even if I'm not *with him* with him. I'm going to try and enjoy it. He's being so nice to me. He's the most popular guy at school, and he's giving *me* attention. That attention may be purely platonic on his part, but I'm still happy to take it.

We get through to the kitchen, and Harper is there with some of her friends. "Rosie, you made it! Wow, you look gorgeous! I knew that top was a must."

I smile at her. "Hi! Thanks again for the shopping trip; you're a lifesaver."

She waves her hand dismissively. "No worries. We had fun. I had a great day." She looks over at Liam. "Doesn't she look gorgeous?"

Right. Harper, going to have to kill you now.

He glances at me. "She does . . . Yeah. Listen, I'm gonna chat with the guys on the team. Will you be okay with Harper, or do you wanna come with me?"

I shake my head and smile at him. "No, I'll be fine."

"Cool." He leans in to say in my ear, "Come and find me if you get bored." The heat of his breath brushes my ear, such an intimate move, and he smells so good.

Harper's eyes widen as he walks away. "Wow, what was that?"

"Behave. It wasn't anything." I dismiss the action even though my heart is racing.

"Hmmm, I'm not too sure about that. Come on. I'll introduce you to my friends."

Two hours later, I've relaxed a ton. I feel a whole lot better about being here. Harper and her friends are lovely. Yeah, sure; they talk about superficial stuff. I mean, who knew you could speak for an hour about contouring? I'm not even sure what contouring is, but they're nice to me. People are being nice to me at a party. So, I'm on cloud nine.

Liam has been over once or twice, and I've caught him watching me a couple of times to make sure that I'm okay. He just wanted me to experience what a party was like. This has proved it; he hasn't been with me much at all. He didn't want my company, just wanted to do something nice for me, and that's okay. I like knowing that he has this lovely side to him, considering we hear so much about his bad side all the time at school.

It's getting near to 10:30. I need to be home by 11. I can't see Liam anywhere. I tell the girls I'm going to look for him so that I can leave. I walk through to the kitchen to see if he's there. A few people are milling around outside. Maybe he's out there? I step out into the cold air, shivering. I need to get my jacket before I leave; it's freezing.

I see Liam with his back to me from where I am and make my way towards him. My eye catches some movement at his waist, a hand . . . A female hand. Liam bends his head, and another hand snakes around his neck. Oh . . . Okay . . . So, he brought me to a party, and now, he's kissing another girl.

Now, yeah, I know I've been saying all night that it's not a date, that he doesn't see me like that, *blah, blah, blah*. Still, I think that, deep down, I wanted it to be one of those fairy tale nights, one that you read about in a romantic novel, that he was going to walk me home, tell me that he liked me, and kiss me. Then, it would all be happily ever after. But this is my life. This is not a romantic fairy tale, and the guy I came with is kissing someone else. The thing is that I have no claim to him whatsoever because that's not what this was supposed to be, so I can't even be upset about it. I inwardly groan when I realize I'm going to have to tell Riley that he copped off. She thought I'd be a buffer to other girls tonight, but she was wrong.

What am I supposed to do now? Mum and Dad would kill me if I walked home on my own. Maybe Russ will still be home. Its 10:30, though. He's probably at the pub with his friends. I'm going to have to ask Dad if he can walk around for me. Not mortifying at all!

I go to step back inside when I barge into someone's chest. "Whoa, you're in a rush. Where are you off to?"

I look up. A tall guy with dark hair is looking down at me, grinning. He's wearing a baseball cap. "I'm sorry . . . I-I didn't see you."

"Don't you worry about that, sweetheart. You can crash into me any time you like." He has a wide grin; he's good-looking but knows it. I think I may have seen him around school but never spoken to him. He carries on. "Where are you going in such a hurry? Come and get a drink with me."

I shake my head. "I can't. Thank you, but I have to go."

"Go? No! You can't go. Come on. It's Saturday night, and it's, like, eight pm. I'm Tim, by the way, and who would you be?"

"Rosie . . . And, nice to meet you, but it's 10:30. I have a curfew."

He frowns. "Well, you're just going to have to give me your number so that I can take you for a drink some other time. What school do you go to? You can't go to Arrowsmith; I would have seen you."

I smile at him. "I do actually, but I'm quite new."

"Wow. You'd think I would have noticed you walking down the halls."

I think there is a strong possibility that this guy has been drinking. I'm not the kind of girl that guys notice when walking down the halls.

"I-I really . . ." I'm interrupted when I feel a hand at my back. I spin around. It's Liam. *What happened to Kissing Girl?*

"Hey, what's up?" he asks.

"Nothing. I just accidentally bumped into Tim here and was saying sorry. It's time for me to go, so I was coming to tell you that I was leaving. But you were busy."

He looks down at his feet, embarrassed.

A girl steps out from behind him, blonde, petite, and pretty—the opposite of me. "Yeah, he *was* busy until he saw you and Tim here causing a commotion."

"Chelsea, pipe down," Liam says and then turns back to me. "I'll walk you home."

That's all I need, him and his bitchy girlfriend walking me home.

"No, it's fine. I'm leaving now; you stay."

"I brought you here, and I'm taking you home. I can come back to the party if I want to. You only live five minutes away."

I try and think of a way to get me out of this awkward situation.

"I'm not taking no for an answer. Tim, entertain Chelsea here for me while I walk Rosie home."

Tim frowns at Liam. "Hey, you trying to cramp my style or what? How many girls do you need to have? One isn't enough? Rosie and I were just getting to know each other, weren't we, sweetheart?" Tim winks at me, and I've got to admit that I kind of like it. I like that he's blatantly flirting with me in front of Liam, too. Maybe it will make him realise that while he doesn't see me in that way, that other guys might. Although even I'm still trying to get my head around that one.

Liam looks probably the most serious I've ever seen him. "I brought Rosie, Tim, so it's my responsibility to get her home safely. If you want to talk to her, you'll have to find her at school. She's in year 11 by the way."

Tim's eyes widen. "Thought she'd be sixth form. Damn, girl. You look older than you are." He shakes his head.

Liam turns to me. "You ready?"

I nod and then turn to Tim and smile. "Nice to meet you."

Tim's face softens; he *is* attractive. "Well, aren't you the sweetest thing?" He leans in to kiss my cheek, just a peck. "I will definitely find you at school."

I feel Liam stiffen at the side of me, and he's giving off a vibe that makes me think Tim is making him mad. Maybe there's a history between them, but Tim hasn't done anything wrong. Liam was just making out with this Chelsea girl in front of me. It's not as if he has any claims on me.

"Come on, Rosie. Tim, look after Chelsea for me," Liam spits out.

Tim nods and winks at Chelsea as though all is right in the world. He isn't picking up on Liam's vibe at all. "It would be my pleasure."

"Ew, don't be so creepy," Chelsea spits then turns the charm on, her face taking on a whole new expression when she looks at Liam, practically batting her eyelashes. "Don't be too long, babe."

"'Kay," Liam says and ushers me through the door. "Come on. We need to get your jacket."

We step outside to make the short journey back to my house. It feels a lot more awkward than on the way to the party if that's possible.

I feel the need to say something. "Thanks for seeing me home; you didn't have to."

"It's fine. I could do with a breather anyway."

Okay. A breather from kissing horrible but pretty girls. Life is hard.

I can't resist; I have to mention it. "You seemed to be having fun."

He looks at me quickly. "What . . . Chelsea? No, I can't seem to get away from her at these parties. Lately, she's everywhere I turn up. Sometimes, it's just easier to go along with what she wants."

"And, it helps that she's gorgeous, of course," I answer.

"You think? I prefer brunettes," he says quietly.

Thank you, God, for giving me brown hair.

"Oh, right. I'm sorry I interrupted you, anyway. I was just going to head home on my own."

"I'd have been upset if you'd done that. Anyway, it looked like Tim was keeping you company."

"What? No, I'd just bumped into him when I was looking for you."

"Watch him; he has a different girl every week."

I laugh. "Sounds like someone else I know."

He frowns. "I'm not as bad as him, I promise you."

"Well . . . I'm sure I'm safe. Can't see me being his next victim."

We lapse back into silence until we arrive at my house. We both come to a standstill. I shiver a little, and he notices. He steps forward and runs his hands up and down my arms. "You're cold. You'd better get inside."

I smile at him, and his eyes go to my mouth. "You have a gorgeous smile. Shame we don't see it much."

"Thanks. I'm working on it." *He thinks I have a gorgeous smile!*

"What did you think of an Arrowsmith High party, then? Have you had a good time? I checked on you a couple of times, and you seemed fine, seemed to be having fun. I didn't want to crowd you while you were relaxed and enjoying yourself."

A warm feeling floods me. He knew I was okay and had left me to enjoy myself.

"You know, it wasn't so bad . . . I'm happy you asked me to go. I think I'll always dread these things, but you showed me that they can still be fun and that some people are nice."

He frowns. "Someone was mean to you in the past, I take it?"

I nod. "Yeah . . . My last school . . . It wasn't great."

"Well, I'm glad I've shown you the other side tonight."

"I owe you . . . Thank you. I had fun. If you ever need any more help with maths, let me know."

His eyes widen as though he's just thought of something. "Actually, can I talk to you about something at school on Monday?"

"Sure . . . Want to talk to me now?" I want to know what it is.

He shakes his head. "No. It's freezing out here. It'll wait. Not on the bus, though. Everyone will be listening; I'll see you at break, maybe at our table in the library?"

Okay. So, we've only been at that table once before, but I love it that he called it our table. It might be freezing outside, but the warm glow all over me is certainly shutting the cold out.

"Yeah, I'll meet you there at first break."

We're both quiet for a minute. Then, I step back, "Thanks again, Liam, and good night. Enjoy the rest of the party."

"Oh, I'm going home now. I never wanted to go back. I'm gonna text Chelsea now to tell her I've gone home. Like I say, she's hard to get away from."

I feel a silly burst of happiness that he's not going back to the party, to her.

"Okay. Well, night then."

I walk inside the house and close the door. I lean my back against it, happy how tonight went, even if his lips have been on someone else. Excitement overtakes me that I have another meeting planned with him. What could he want to see me about? I go to bed with a thousand possibilities whirring around my mind.

Chapter Three

Liam

The bell sounds, and I pack up. I need to get to the library; we only have 20 minutes for break, and it's all the way on the other side of the school.

I rush out and start to cross the year 11 yard when I hear someone call my name.

"Liam, wait up." It's Mark.

"Hey, dude. What's up? I have somewhere I need to be."

"This Rosie chick, the one that you took to the party on Saturday, can you give me her number?"

I shake my head. "No, dude. Leave her be; she's not your type."

"Come on . . . All girls are my type. She had a fine body, that one. Think she's a 21-year-old trapped in the body of a schoolgirl. You know what I'm sayin'?"

I take a deep breath. *Keep your cool, Liam.* "Yeah, I get it, but leave her be."

"Why? You wanting to cut a slice of that cake for yourself?"

I can feel the rage building inside me. I don't like girls being disrespected, but I especially don't like him talking about Rosie that way. She has done nothing to deserve it. She doesn't flaunt herself about, trying to get attention; she's a class act.

"Tim, seriously. Leave it."

"Ah, you do. Or have you already? Doesn't take long with you, does it? Well, knowing what you're like, you'll probably be done with her in a week. So, throw me a bone when you're done, will you, and give me her number?"

Right. That's it. How dare he talk about her that way! I grab him by the collar and push him up against the wall. "You *ever* talk about her like that again, and you will have me to answer to. You get it?"

"Wow! Wow. I was only asking; I didn't know you and she were a thing. I thought, on Saturday, you were with Chelsea. So, I just presumed..."

"Well, don't presume. Don't give her another thought, okay?"

He holds his hands up. "Okay. Okay. Sorry, dude. But seriously, let me go now, or we are going to have problems." His tone has turned serious. I don't care. I've gone past the point of caring. But then, I remember Rosie is waiting at the library for me. I need to go. I exhale and release him.

"Whatever," I say and walk away towards the library.

I look at the time. I needed to be there five minutes ago. *Idiot.* I hated hearing him talk about Rosie that way, though. I mean, it's not just because it's Rosie. For all my faults, I don't like girls being talked about that way.

Still, pinning a member of my basketball team up against a wall was probably a dumb move. That's why I'm meeting Rosie in the first place, after all. I need her to help me with my reputation. At this point, I'm about one detention away from suspension. Next is expulsion. Although, maybe if I get expelled from somewhere, my parents might remember I'm alive.

Yeah, right. It would take a lot more than that. I can't even remember the last time I saw my dad. He works in every country in the world except this one. Mum is just as bad; I think the last time I saw her was three days ago. She is the first one at the office and the last one to leave. I barely even see her. A lot of the guys at school think I'm lucky. I've got money—as much of it as I want—and I'm left to my own devices all the time with no parent breathing down my neck. It's not as much fun as it seems on paper. Kind of makes me feel not wanted. Pretty much alone. It sucks actually . . . I hate it.

I can't get expelled, though. I like it here. I have such a good thing going with Mr. Trent in wood tech. I'm so grateful that he lets me hang there and do my own projects. I'd be mad to mess that up; it's the only thing that keeps me sane. Why can't I just keep out of trouble? My temper gets the better of me every single time. I just can't seem to control it. I feel so angry all the time. But Rosie? What has she done to anyone? Nothing. Everyone just liked what they saw—big time—on Saturday. She is something to look at alright. She's not "in your face" glamorous like so many of the girls at this school are even though they claim they're not. She is . . . well . . . beautiful, I guess, with that hair and those gorgeous eyes. Those lips of hers...Jeez, they are made to be kissed. Not by me, though. No way. I like to hang out with girls, like their company, do a little making out, but I'm not down for a relationship. Ever. If what my parents have got is anything to go by, I don't think I'll ever want to bother. What's the point? Apart from the warmth of a soft, female body anyway, and I can get that any time I want.

I walk into the library and see her sitting at our table. I dump my backpack on the table, making her jump. She was in her head. I wonder what she was thinking about. I'm hoping that this proposition I have for her will be as beneficial for her as it will be for me, or I'll never get her to agree. I, at least, have to make it sound that way.

"Oh, hey. I didn't see you come in." She smiles at me. I like her smile.

I sit down next to her. "Sorry I'm late. I ran into a bit of trouble." I decide not to tell her that it may have been about her.

She sighs. "Is it me, or are you always running into trouble?"

I flash her a grin. "So, you keep tabs on me, do you?"

"Oh, yeah. It's hard not to; you're always top news at this school, you know."

I raise my eyebrows. "Am I? All good, I hope."

She taps her chin as though in thought. "Well, let's see. There are the girls who practically fall at your feet when you walk past, there are all the guys that think you're so cool they want to be you, and then there are all the sensible ones—like me—who are thankful that they don't get into as much trouble as you do."

I put my hand on my chest. "I'm hurt. I thought you'd be one of the girls that swoons over me."

She blushes; I love making her blush. I feel like it's cruel to want to make her blush, but I can't help myself. Maybe if I've embarrassed her, then there's some truth in it? I hope not. If she has a thing for me, this plan I have won't work at all. Attraction and feelings can't get in the way.

"No . . . I think you get enough attention." Her voice is quiet. She clears her throat and speaks louder this time. "So, what did you want to talk to me about? The bell is going to ring for the end of break in five minutes or so."

"Er, yeah . . . I have something I want to ask you. Now, don't say no straight away. It may sound crazy, but there's a method in my madness. And, I think it will help us both out."

"Oh-kay. . . " She looks terrified.

I give a half-laugh. "Relax. I'm not suggesting we go on a killing spree or anything." I take a deep breath. "I was wondering if you would maybe hang out with me, be seen with me, kind of pretend to be my girlfriend."

Her eyes widen, and she gasps. "What? Are you crazy? Why?"

31

I shrug. "I have my reasons . . . I came up with the idea when you helped me with maths the other day. I'm in trouble, and I keep getting in trouble. I'm nearing expulsion; I just know it, and I just can't seem to keep my nose clean."

"And, you think being around me will help you be good?"

I scrunch my nose up in a way I know the girls find cute. I'm pulling out all the stops here. "Well, kind of. You can help me with homework, and we can hang out. You're so squeaky clean and smart that when all the teachers find out we're an item, they'll think I'm calming down. Plus, my work will be improving, so they'll back off."

She is silent, staring at me like I've grown another head.

I lean into her. "Say something."

She shakes her head a little as though she's been talking to herself. "I can see what you're saying, that you might get everyone to back off because I'm such a goody-goody."

"No . . . I didn't mean . . ." Offending her is not the way to go.

She raises her hand to stop me. "It's okay. I *am* a goody-goody and absolutely fine with that." She carries on. "But at the risk of sounding ruthless and cold, apart from just doing an angelic good deed, what would be in it for me?"

She thinks I can't help her; how wrong she is. I'm good at reading people, and I can read her like a book. She oozes insecurity and unhappiness. I can change that.

"Well, I'm kinda popular." I smile at her.

She rolls her eyes at me, and I chuckle. "inNo offence, but you blend into the crowd. I get the feeling that's because you want to blend in. You don't want to be seen. It doesn't take a genius to work out that girls at your other school had a problem with you. I don't know the details—and I don't need to—but it doesn't need to be like that here. You don't need to blend in. You can be whoever the hell you want to be. No one knows you. Whoever was mean to you, they're not here now. I can help you. You can come to parties with me and meet people instead of hiding away all the time."

She looks stunned and even more terrified than she did five minutes ago. "How-How did you figure all that out about me?"

I shrug. "I'm good at reading people. Always have been."

She clears her throat and looks at her hands on the table. Is she upset? Crap! Have I gone too far?

She looks up at me with tears in her eyes. I didn't think I'd been mean or said anything that wasn't true. Maybe the truth hurts, or maybe this girl has been through the wringer and is still hurting.

"I'm sorry; I didn't mean to upset you. I just figured that I could help, help you fit in or whatever, and one thing I am good at is popularity. I figured we could scratch each other's backs. And, if you help me, you'll *definitely* go to heaven."

She laughs, and her whole face changes. Doesn't she know how pretty she is? I'm relieved that I haven't made her cry.

"Can I think about it? An offer like this is the last thing I thought was going to come out of your mouth. I thought you were going to ask me to do your history homework or something."

"I'm not that bad." I put on an affronted voice.

She gives me the look, the look that women perfect from a very early age, the one that says, *"Really?"*.

"Okay. Fine. Maybe I am that bad sometimes, but that is why you are going to make me a changed man."

"We'll see. Can I let you know after school?"

I nod. "Sure." Then, I remember I'm in wood tech after school. "Come to the wood tech lab; I'm there after school."

"You got detention in tech?" she asks.

"Now, I'm hurt. No, I have not. Just come; I'll show you what I do there." I figure if I show her that I'm not all bad, that I do have some substance, then she'll agree.

"Okay. I'll see you there after school before I go for the bus."

I nod and stand up, giving her a mini bow and one of my grins that I know works well with all the ladies. Gotta work with what I've got.

"See you later." I turn and leave just as the bell rings. That'll give her some food for thought.

*****

The final bell goes. Thank God. Maths seriously melts my brain. I pack up and make my way over to Tech. I bet everyone on the bus always presumes I'm in detention when I don't make it. I look around for Rosie; no sign. That can't be good. I felt for sure she would agree. Maybe there's time yet; I did get out of maths pretty swiftly.

I walk into wood tech and inhale. The smell of wood automatically calms me. I wish I could live in this lab. Everyone has their special talent, right? Mine is wood. I love to carve it, making it into something, something worthwhile. There is nothing like getting a plain old piece of wood and turning it into something special. The satisfaction it gives me is way more than passing any maths test could ever provide. Unfortunately, the maths and other subjects need to be passed, too. It's not that I'm bad at math; I just can't be bothered with it. It's just a necessary evil. I'm only good at the things I'm interested in.

Mr. Trent, my wood tech teacher and absolutely the coolest teacher ever, comes around the corner while looking down at a notebook; he doesn't notice I'm in the room.

"Sir."

His head snaps up. "Liam! I didn't hear you come in. You are going to put me in an early grave!"

I laugh. "Sorry, sir. Am I alright to carry on with my project?"

"Of course, you can; you know where it is. I'll be here for a couple of hours yet. This teaching gig is alright until it comes to all the paperwork that goes with it."

"Thanks, sir." I set my things down and go to get my project. As I turn back to my workbench, I see Rosie standing there. Jeez, I understand what Mr. Trent meant now; she scared me half to death. I feel hope rise in my chest at the thought of her being here to say yes.

"Hey! What are you, a stealth ninja or something? I didn't hear you come in."

She smiles and looks down at my hands. "Sorry. What are you doing here? Are you finishing something off?" She takes a step towards me.

I shake my head. "No. I come here to hang out. Mr. Trent is cool. He knows how much I love to do this kind of stuff, so he lets me come back here after school whenever he's staying late."

She looks up at me, her face soft. "So, when everyone on the bus thinks you're in detention, you're actually here?"

I grimace. "Well, sometimes. A lot of the time, I'm *actually* in detention, but sometimes, I'm here. I come here at lunch, too, occasionally."

She points to the wood in my hand. "What are you making?"

I hold up something that pretty much just looks like a block of wood at the moment. "This is going to be a perfect rose, carved out of a single piece of wood."

Her eyes widen. "Wow. So, you're really good?"

"I'm okay. I like to do it; it's relaxing." And, I definitely need that.

"I didn't think you could get any more relaxed."

"You'd be surprised," I say sadly.

"I'd love to see it when it's finished." My chest tightens; I love that she wants to see it. Apart from Mr. Trent, no one has any interest in this stuff.

"I don't show my creations around," I lean in closer to her, "but I might make an exception as long as you don't tell anyone my dark secret."

She smiles at me.

Don't look at her mouth; don't look at her mouth. She has the most gorgeous, plump lips. I just want to bite them. *What? Where did that come from?* The last thing I need is to feel an attraction for this girl. Relationships are a big fat no for me. This girl is *definitely* the relationship type, too. If she were the type for a one-night kissing fest, though, that would be some night.

"My lips are sealed."

Damn! Why did she have to mention her lips?

I change the subject before my mind goes in the gutter. "Have you thought about my proposition?"

She flushes again; it's so easy to embarrass her.

"I have. I-I might be mad, but yeah. Okay. Let's give it a go."

"Really?" I was hoping for a yes, but I didn't really expect one.

She nods. "Can't hurt, right? We both get to help each other. God knows I need help."

I grin at her. "Great! We'll need to go over details and things. Do you want to meet up tonight? Everyone always goes over to the skate park at Westpoint and hangs around there; it's not very exciting, but everyone will think it's a date. It's the place to be seen."

There's that terrified look again. "I guess I could. It's not far from my house, so I can walk."

I shake my head. "No way. It'll be dark. I will call for you; we'll walk there together."

She looks relieved. "Oh, alright. Thanks. What time shall I be ready?"

"I'll come at seven. Is that okay?" I can't remember the last time I went on a date, even if it was fake.

"Sure. That's fine. I had better go, or I'll miss the bus." She gives me a little wave and leaves. I watch the door close behind her. A boring night of staying in alone just got a whole lot more appealing.

Chapter Four

Rosie

My life is so surreal right now.

Am I really going to be in a relationship with the hottest guy in school? Alright, so it might be a fake one, but still . . .

I'm still reeling over this from lunchtime when he asked me. I've been able to think about nothing else all afternoon. I went from yes to no to yes about 500 times. I finally settled on yes. I'm trying to go with the "you only live once" attitude and make myself do things I wouldn't normally do. This falls into that category for sure. I think about him in wood tech now, working away on that wood. Everyone thinks he's in trouble when he's been going in there for goodness knows how long to work on projects. It makes my heart hurt to think of him in there, concentrating, taking care in what he's doing.

I pick up my pace, hoping that I haven't missed the bus. I hurry around the corner, relieved that the bus is still there. I was pushing it by going to see Liam.

Tony gives me a nod. "Nearly went without you then, sweetheart. Come on."

I smile at him gratefully. "Thanks, Tony." I sit down next to Riley. My stomach starts to churn at the thought of what I have to tell her.

"Where have you been? Tony should have set off five minutes ago but said he'd wait for you. I assured him that hell would freeze over before you got a detention."

I give a short laugh. She's right; I would die before getting detention.

"Riley, I have to tell you something. You won't believe what's happened. I don't even know where to start."

"Oooh! Sounds good, so spill."

I look around the bus. The twins are talking to Harper, the scary girl, that I now know is called Kinsley, has her headphones in as usual, and Charlie is watching something on his phone. I have to tell Riley the truth; I owe it to her, and I know I can trust her. I need someone to talk to about it all. No one else can know, though.

"Okay. But you have to keep your voice down, and you can't tell anyone."

She wriggles in her seat a little. "Come on; the anticipation is killing me!"

"I'm serious. Do you promise this will not go any further?"

"I promise. Now, tell me."

I chicken out. I can't tell her right now, because if someone overhears, that will be it; it will be over before it has even started.

"No. I can't here. What are you doing when we get home? Are you training tonight?"

"No, it's Monday; I have Mondays off. Shall I come back to yours with you?"

I nod. "Yeah. Come and hang. No one will be in anyway. Oh, my brother might be there."

"Oooh, I finally get to meet Russ, do I?"

I roll my eyes. "Don't get too excited; you might get a grunt off him, but that'll be it. He's so grumpy lately."

"I'm still dying to meet him. I'll message my dad now to let him know I'll be late."

"Yeah, it won't be too late. I-I have things to do later." *Oh, God. Please be okay with it.*

Her head snaps up. "What do you have to do later?"

"Shh . . . that's part of my news."

"Okay. Tony had better drive fast tonight or else."

We get to my house, and I let us in. "Hello? Anyone home?"

Sky comes bounding towards me. Riley has met her before; they love each other. It's my favourite part of the day, getting in and seeing her, her tail wagging. She is so happy to see me. Her unconditional love swells my heart every time.

I bend down and stroke my girl while she licks me, unable to control her excitement. Russ shouts from somewhere; I think the kitchen. "Yeah. Me. You okay?"

He appears around the door of the kitchen and looks at me and then his eyes go to Riley. He looks at her for a second longer than is polite and then looks back at me. "You okay?" he asks again.

"Yeah. This is Riley, my friend from school."

He does a chin lift but doesn't smile. "Hey."

Jeez, don't go all out, Russ.

I look over at Riley. She looks like a deer caught in headlights. I've never seen her stand still for longer than two seconds.

"Okay. We're hanging out upstairs for a while."

He nods. "Fine. Mum put dinner in the slow cooker, so it's ready whenever you want it."

"Oh, cool. I'll have some in a while. I'm going out later," I say quickly.

"I think she has a date." Riley decides to speak. *Great.*

"Oh, yeah? With that guy, Liam, again?"

I glance at Riley then back to Russ. "Never you mind."

He nods and then turns to Riley. "You going with them?"

Why is he asking her that? Obviously not.

She is suddenly struck dumb. I know that to other girls that aren't his sister, Russ is hot. He's tall, broad, and 18 with dark hair and blue eyes. So, it looks like I've lost Riley to the curse of my big brother.

"Er, um..." she stutters and blushes. I try not to laugh at her, falling to pieces for my big brother.

I elbow her to come back onto our planet. "No, she's not. Why?"

He shakes his head. "No reason . . . just wondered." He looks at her again; she just stares at him. *Interesting.*

I don't hang around. "Okay. Come on, chatterbox. We're going upstairs."

I drag her up to my room, and she flops down on my bed.

"Oh, my God. How gorgeous is your brother?" she practically pants.

I screw my nose up in disgust. "Ew! He's not; he's my brother, and don't even think about it. He would chew you up and spit you out. He's nearly 19 and going to Uni, and he's really grumpy."

"Hmmm, I bet I could cheer him up."

"Right. Ew, and stop it. Never say anything like that again." I throw a pillow at her. "Although, I do think he showed you more interest than he does anything else right now. I think he might fancy you."

Her eyes light up. "You think?"

I shake my head. "Seriously, don't let your head go there."

"Sorry. Right. Come on; spill. What is going on?"

"Okay. So, I told you Liam wanted to meet me at break, that he wanted to ask me something?"

"Yeah, you thought it was help with schoolwork."

I shoot her a look. "It was more than that. I'm going to help him with schoolwork, but quite a bit more, too."

A look of concern flashes over her face, but then, it's gone in an instant.

"God, Riley. I hope you will be okay with this, because I kind of agreed already."

"Okay. What did he want, then?"

I fill her in on everything. I don't tell her the part about him spending time in wood tech; I have a feeling he doesn't want that to be common knowledge. When I've told her everything, she just stares at me.

"So, come on; say something."

"Do you think this is a good idea?" she says quietly.

"Well, I'm not sure if I'm honest, but I promised myself when I started this school that I'd push myself to the limit and try new things. So, this is me trying new things. I'm just hoping you are okay with it."

She studies me. "Do you not think it will get out of hand, spending all this time with him? That you might get feelings for him?"

I had thought about this; I'm attracted to him. Very attracted. I'm just hoping that I can keep a lid on it. The last thing I want Liam to know is how much I fancy him.

"I don't want a boyfriend; he's just trying to get me to fit in more at school. Truth is, Riley, I know I've told you a little, but I had an ordeal at my last school. It was, like, *really bad*, and I got depressed and withdrawn from life a bit, you know? So, I need to push myself, do things I wouldn't normally do. I think he's attractive, sure, but can you see me falling for the bad guy? Trust me; a boyfriend is the last thing I need right now. And, Liam? I bet the word 'girlfriend' terrifies him. He's only interested in hook-ups. I'll only do it if you're okay with it."

She doesn't look convinced. "I guess it's okay. I just don't want you to get hurt."

I shake my head. "I won't fall for him; I just like that I get to help him out, and maybe he can show me how to relax and mix better in the meantime."

"We'll see, but I can't help but be worried that this will end in tears. But yeah. I'm okay with it. It's not like he and I would ever go out, anyway; he doesn't see me in that way."

I grin and go over to hug her. "He's blind, 'cos you're amazing."

She rolls her eyes. "Yeah, whatever. So, where are you going tonight?"

I feel sick at the thought of where I'm going tonight. It's my worst nightmare. "He wants me to go to the skate park, said a bunch of them hang out there.

Honestly, I'd rather do anything but hang out there. It's not my idea of fun, but he said it would be a good place to be seen together. Then, everyone will see that we're a thing."

She sighs. "I hope you're sure about this."

I shake my head. "I'm not; I'm terrified, but I think I need to do this, prove to myself that I'm normal or whatever. Obviously, I need therapy." I give an unconvincing laugh. "I think I just need to prove to myself that they didn't win, that I've got the confidence to do this."

She looks at me softly. "I'm sorry you went through that, Rosie. You do what you need to do. Just be careful, okay?"

I'm relieved. That is kind of like getting her blessing. "I will; promise."
*****

Two hours later, I'm walking to the park with Liam. He's changed out of his school uniform, and he's wearing dark blue jeans with a sea blue t-shirt and a jumper. I'm sure he knows that wearing that colour makes his eyes look 10 times brighter.

I decided on jeans, my biker boots, and biker jacket with my hair down and a long-sleeved top. It's a Monday night; I don't want to look as though I've made an effort, tried too hard. I've put on a little makeup, some mascara and bronzer. I'm so nervous. This "pushing myself out of my comfort zone" thing doesn't feel fun at all. It's horrible. I could be at home on my bed, watching TV in my pyjamas, Sky lying next to me. My safe place. But I'm so far away from my safe place right now.

We talk about nothing important. When we reach the park, I see a crowd from school milling around.

"You ready for this?" he asks, smiling.

Those eyes of his are doing the crinkly thing at the corners. He could be asking me if I'm ready to throw myself under a bus, and I'd agree with him right now.

I give him a small smile. "Let's do it."

He stops walking and holds his hand out. What does he want? "What?"

He chuckles. "You're gonna have to hold my hand. You know that hand-holding, cuddling, and stuff goes with this deal, right?"

I swallow; I mean, I know what you do when you're boyfriend and girlfriend, but the fact that I'll be doing that with Liam makes my anxiety spike but also sparks excitement, too.

"I guess; I suppose that's what we can decide on tonight, what we will do and won't do . . . "

He nods. "Well, yeah. But this is a given. We might as well make a statement."

I take a deep breath and place my hand in his, every nerve ending in my palm and fingers coming alive, feeling as though I've plugged my fingers into an electrical socket. I look up. Based on the look on his face, he feels it, too.

He clears his throat. "Come on."

We walk over to the crowd, my nerves playing a fine tune up and down my body. I'm so out of my comfort zone right now. As we approach, one by one, they start to notice us. I feel like I'm in one of those movie scenes where time stands still, and everyone stops what they're doing. Of course, it isn't like that, just my overactive imagination. I'm worried that I'm going to see my dinner again. Why did I agree to do this? They're all looking at me. I look at Liam to find him watching me.

"You okay?" he asks. Maybe I actually *look* like I'm going to see my dinner again.

I nod. "Yeah. Just . . . Well, this is all new for me. I'm nervous." I hate admitting it to him, but I need an ally here tonight.

He gives me a gentle smile. He is so beautiful. "You don't need to be nervous; I'll be with you. Honestly, they're okay. No one will be mean to you. I bet you didn't know that this was going on while you were at home, doing your homework."

Okay, Liam. Way to point out that I'm sad and have no life.

"No, I didn't. Everyone is going to be so shocked. This has happened, literally, in one afternoon. There are going to be a lot of questions."

He shrugs. "We might as well make it public as soon as possible. We'll go over, talk a while, then you and I will go and sit somewhere, just the two of us. Trust me . . . "

I nod and exhale slowly. He gives a nod to some of the guys in the group. I recognise them but don't know them. The girls are the ones that were with Harper at the party. One smiles at me, so I give her a little wave.

He leans in to say in my ear, "They're the best form of communication you can have; this will be all around the school tomorrow."

I can't think about that. All I can think about is how close his mouth is to my ear, how I can feel his hot breath on my cheek, and how his aftershave is doing strange things to my senses. He put on aftershave for me. Why does that make me feel really good? He made an effort just for little old me.

"I guess there's no turning back now."

"Nope. Come on. Let's do this."

One of the guys greets us, "Liam! How's it going?" He gives him some sort of guy handshake and then looks at me. I don't know who he is.

"Good. Kane, this is Rosie."

"Hey, Rosie. I've seen you around; you're new, right?"

I nod. "Yeah. Hi. I just started in September."

"Cool, but you know you're with the bad boy, right? You need to be careful about your reputation."

I can tell he's joking. He looks over at Liam and winks. Liam laughs. My heart stops. I've never seen him properly laugh before; it's the most fantastic sight and sound.

"As long as he's not bad to me." I smile at Kane.

He looks over to Liam. "How did you get her to agree to go out with you?"

Liam squeezes my hand. "Come on, dude. You know that *they* come to *me*."

I gasp and slap him. "I did not!"

Liam chuckles and shakes his head. "No. For once, I did the asking."

"Well, that's a first." He turns to me. "Welcome to the crew, Rosie; it's all very boring here, but it's somewhere to hang.There aren't many places to meet up at night."

I nod and smile. "Thanks."

We talk to a few of the others. Some just glance my way but don't ask anything. Some of the guys come outright and ask what's going on, so he tells them that we're seeing each other. They all look surprised, but no one is nasty. Harper's friends come over, being friendly. I think I see admiration in their eyes that I'm with Liam. They're probably wondering how I've managed to bag him. I mean, he wasn't wrong before; all the girls do seem to have a thing for him. I get why, though. The bad boy thing, the way he looks, moves, carries himself. He is good to look at, but also, he omits an aura that oozes confidence. He commands a room or even a park when he walks into it. What must it be like to have so much confidence? I guess that is what makes him so attractive to all the girls. It helps that he's tall, broad, and has gorgeous blue eyes with dark hair, but as a whole, he's a pretty irresistible package. I realise I've been staring at him for a while, and he looks down at me and holds my gaze. It's like he can read my mind, that I was thinking all that about him. A slow, lazy smile appears on his face. This guy is going to break my heart. If I let him, that is.

He leans close to me. "Come on. Let's go have a walk and a chat on our own."

He pulls me off, away from the crowd.

"So, where do we start?" he asks, a twinkle in his eye.

"I don't know. How did you think that went, then? With your friends?"

43

He shrugs. "Fine."

"Do you think they believed us?"

"Why wouldn't they?"

He can't think this is an easy sell. "Well, because... You know, we're so different. I'm, well, me, and you're..."

"What am I, Rosie?" He has a mischievous look on his face.

"Why do I get the feeling that you are loving seeing me squirm?" I ask him.

He chuckles. "I'm sorry. I've never seen anyone look so uncomfortable. Just relax. I don't bite. Well, unless you want me to?"

My face fires up on cue at his comment.

"God, I'm sorry. I can't help my mouth. Forget I said that. I was joking around, but I'm not helping. So, how shall we do this? Tomorrow, on the bus, Harper will have already heard the news, so if you meet me at the bus stop and come and stand close to me, maybe hold my hand, then no one will think it's weird."

"But you're always late," I say doubtfully.

"I won't be. I promise. I'll be early. I mean, I'll be excited to see my new girlfriend, won't I?"

"I don't think anyone would believe that."

"What do you mean?"

"Like you'd ever be excited to go out with me." I instantly regret saying that as soon as it's out of my mouth. It sounds like I'm fishing for compliments; I'm really not. I don't believe that anyone would think we were a real couple. He is way out of my league.

"What exactly is that supposed to mean?" There's a hint of anger creeping into his voice.

I sigh. "I just think this is going to be a hard sell, that's all. You and me. No one is going to think that you would give me a second look. You're . . . Well, you're popular and . . . good looking." I say the "good looking" part quietly so that he can hardly hear. *This is mortifying.*

"And, you are . . .?"

"Don't make me say it. This is embarrassing enough. Let's just say that no one will put the two of us together."

"You are so weird, Rosie."

I'm taken aback. "Wow. Thanks."

"I'm sorry. There's that mouth of mine again. I just mean that I don't think you see what everyone else sees. You have a distorted view of yourself. I don't get it. You are gorgeous but in a way that doesn't make you conceited; you have no idea. I guess that's because you don't think you're gorgeous. There is so much wonderful stuff about you, and then, there's the fact that you're a genius, too. You're a catch."

I snort. *Attractive, Rosie*. "And, that right there is the reason that everyone will think that you're with me? The fact that I'm smart?"

He stops walking, turns to face me, and grabs my other hand so that he's holding them both. My brain goes on alert, trying to make sense of what is happening. He starts to stroke his thumbs along my hands, leaving a tingle in their wake. I wish he didn't have this effect on me. His touch is giving me goosebumps.

"Well, we will just have to put on such a good performance that no one will be questioning why I'm with you." He pulls me over to sit with him on a nearby bench.

I smile. "You're a lot nicer, you know, than I thought you were when I first met you on the bus."

"I can be," he says, sounding wary.

"Why do you get into so much trouble at school?" I have to ask. He seems so lovely but yet always in trouble. I don't get it.

His face closes down. This is obviously not a subject he wants to discuss. He shrugs. "Dunno, really. Does it matter?"

I nod. "If you want to pass your exams, yeah. What are you doing after we finish year 11?"

"I want an apprenticeship in woodwork, but I need to pass maths for that."

"So, that's why you need help from me?"

He nods. "Yeah. It's important to me."

"You love doing that stuff, don't you?"

His eyes light up. "I do. I love making useful things out of something that was just a block of wood, you know? And, it's so relaxing. I can have a head full of crap, but it just melts away when I'm doing that, like therapy, I guess. Do you have anything like that?"

"The only thing that makes me feel like that, so happy, is spending time with Sky, my dog. I just love her. With all the things that went on at school last year, she was always there for me, always my friend, you know? I know it sounds stupid; she's a dog, but she's always happy to see me and has such unconditional love. No human has unconditional love."

He smiles at me warmly. "I like that you have that."

"She's the best, a rescue German Shepherd, but she's huge. We think there's another breed thrown in there, too, but she's friendly. You'll have to meet her sometime."

45

"I'd like that. So, what's the next plan of action? You wanna come to my place tomorrow night to study? I have basketball practice, but I could come to yours afterwards. I have a car that picks me up when we have practice, so I can just swing by and get you. Are you free?"

I nod. "I'm free tomorrow night, yeah. Will it be okay with your parents?"

Something flashes in his eyes. It looks like he's angry. But then, he shakes his head, and it's gone. "Dad works away; I never see him, and Mum works long hours. She only gets in around nine. We'll be done by then anyway. As long as you don't mind being in the house alone with me."

I shake my head. "No, I don't mind. It's not like you're going to try anything as is it." I laugh.

"There you go again. We need to get you over this negative opinion of yourself, don't we?"

"Good luck with that." *After years of hearing you're fat, ugly, and worthless, how are you supposed to think otherwise?*

"Okay. So, I'll see you tomorrow. Connor is having another party on Saturday, so can you come to that with me?"

I shake my head. "Oh, my God. I swear that's all he ever does."

He chuckles. "Yeah, but at least we all have somewhere to go." He looks serious suddenly. "We need to talk about what we can do and what you're not comfortable with."

I swallow. I don't like where this is going. "Okay . . . What do you think I should be comfortable with?"

He smiles and shakes his head. "What about kissing? Do you think you'd be okay kissing me?" He looks down to my mouth as he says it. My tongue darts out to lick my upper lip; an instinct, I suppose, while they're under scrutinization. His eyes darken as he looks up at me. "Rosi, I--"

"Liam." A guy comes into view, holding the hand of a girl I haven't seen before. I guess they wanted privacy, but I get the feeling it wasn't to chat like Liam and me. I sigh, relieved that he, whoever he is, broke the tension between us. It felt intense for a moment there.

The guy walks over to us. We watch the girl kiss him on the cheek and then run back to the crowd to join her friends. He does a stupid handshake thing with Liam, too.

"Hey, Gaz. How's it going?"

Gaz nods. "Yeah . . . Good. What about you? Punching above your weight with this lovely thing again?" He must have seen us at the party.

He looks over at me. "I'm Gaz. I'm on the team with Liam here, and he has been keeping you a secret. I think I know why."

Oh, God. Does he think Liam should be ashamed of being seen with me?

Liam looks over at me and smiles. "Yeah. This is Rosie. She has crazily agreed to go out with me again, so like I'm not gonna say no."

Gaz laughs. "Yeah. She must be nuts. Are you new?"

I nod. "Yeah. Just started this September."

"I thought I hadn't seen you around. Think I'd have noticed you."

What does he mean by that?

"Wow. I *know* you are not hitting on my date, dude."

Gaz throws his arms up in mock surrender. "Sorry. I can't help it; it just comes naturally."

Liam laughs. "Right. Well, get lost, then, and leave us to it."

Gaz turns to me and gives me a little bow. "Lovely to meet you, Rosie." Then, he walks away.

Liam looks at me and raises an eyebrow.

"What?" I ask.

"He thinks you're hot," he states.

"No, he doesn't. He was just flirting; he probably does it with everyone."

He shakes his head. "This is gonna be harder than I thought. Not the 'getting you to fit in with everyone' part; the 'getting you to believe in yourself enough to do it' part."

Maybe he's right. He does have his work cut out. I smile at him. "Anyway, where were we? Saturday? Yes, I can come."

He nudges my shoulder. "We weren't there, and you know it. But I'll let it go for now."

Phew. Good. Because I didn't know what I was going to say. I've never kissed a guy before. He's obviously a professional kisser. I don't want to seem like a total amateur. Surely, people don't need to see us kissing.

"Okay. So, I'll see you around at school?"

"Yeah. I'll just hang out with you at school as much as I can. All the teachers will suddenly think I'm an angel if you will give me your time. Plus, if I hang with you, it will keep me out of trouble."

"How do you know? Maybe I go for a smoke around the back of the science building then make out with a different boy every day before going back to class."

He throws his head back and laughs. "Now I *know* your joking."

47

I revel in the moment and the beauty that is watching him laugh. I guess tomorrow at school will be the real test for both of us.

Chapter Five

Rosie

Meet me at the bus stop. I'm already here. Impressed?

A text message from Liam. Wow. I *am* impressed. I'm always early, and I'm a couple of minutes away from the stop yet. He must be trying hard. I need to tell him that Riley knows. I message him back:

I am impressed. Btw, I've told Riley that it isn't real. We can trust her.

As I turn the corner, I see him standing there, looking on his phone. He's so hot. It's like every girl's dream is standing there, and he's going to be paying attention to *me*. Alright, not real attention, but still. It's something to dream about tonight. How many girls get to live out their fantasy? Although, in my fantasy, there is a lot of kissing. I've thought about what he said last night like a hundred times, thought of what it must be like to kiss him. I bet he's kissed lots of girls. I already caught him kissing one. I wonder how far he's gone with a girl, if kissing is where it has stopped or if there's more. I haven't even kissed a boy. He's probably done it all.

As I walk towards him, he sees me, and a slow smile spreads over his face. It's November, but I feel like the sun has just come out. I've made a little more effort today with my appearance for school. I mean, come on; I'm going to be the girlfriend of the hottest guy in school. I should at least try to look the part. I have my hair mostly down—I ran straighteners over it this morning—and put on some mascara and bronzer, so it doesn't look like I've got any on. Oh, and I'm wearing lip gloss, too. This keeping-up-appearances business is already exhausting. Having to get up an extra hour earlier just to work on my appearance is not my idea of fun.

"Morning, boyfriend," I say, giving him a grin.

"Hey, girlfriend. Come here." Wow . . . Said like that, how can I resist?

When I reach him, he places his hand on my neck, resting the weight of his arm on my shoulder.

"How are you doing this morning?" His voice is so rough and gravelly, as though he's only just woken up. He steps even closer to me, our bodies only an inch or so from touching. It's freezing, but suddenly, I feel hot. He smells so good, aftershave and that other smell which I now know to be a wood smell. Does he work on it at home, too?

"You know," he says in a low voice, "that you were the last person I saw before I went to bed last night, and you're the first person I've seen since I got up? I'm sure that practically makes us married."

I struggle to breathe. I have to remind myself to take a breath in. The way he's looking at me, touching me, and saying those words, it feels so real. I have to remind myself this is all fake. The reason I'm doing this is to help me be who I want to be. I need to not fall for the bad boy while I'm doing it. Getting myself into trouble and noticed for all the wrong reasons is not the way I want to go.

"I think you've missed out on a big chunk of what being married involves." My eyes widen when I realise what I've implied. "I-I don't mean that's what I want. Oh-oh God... Never mind."

He chuckles, and his head dips into me a little more. "I like you in the morning. You're all dizzy and in another world. You might be the brainiest person in year 11, but it takes that amazing brain of yours a while to wake up. Good to know you're not perfect!"

I stick my tongue out at him playfully, and he looks down at my mouth. He makes a growling sound. "Don't draw my attention to that mouth of yours."

I swallow, about to retort with something light when I hear, "Oh, my God. It's true!"

He moves his hand away from my neck and slides it around my shoulder, drawing me into him and turning us both towards the voice. Harper.

"Hey, Harper," I say. "Happy Tuesday!"

"Never mind happy Tuesday! When were you going to tell me that you two are a thing?"

I feel bad not telling Harper the truth. I consider her a friend now, but gossip is her favourite pastime. How would she keep it in? If she knew this was fake, she'd have to tell the whole world.

"Yeah. It kind of happened fast. Like, yesterday fast," Liam says, smiling.

She narrows her eyes at him. "Now, you listen to me, mister. You be nice to her. I know what you're like; you have a different girl every week. There should be a no fraternising rule on this bus, seeing as we all have to get the bus together every day. I don't want her crying next week. Got that?"

He salutes her with his other hand. "Sir, yes, sir!"

She glares at him a minute longer then turns to me. "So, tell all."

Oh, God.

They all turn up one by one. Kinsley, looking at us both together, just shakes her head and gets on the bus.

Then, the twins turn up, and Harper shouts to them, "I told you so," while pointing at us.

Charlie, next, just turns up with a big grin on his face, looking at us both. "A little birdie told me." He points to Harper. *Is there anyone she hasn't told?*

Riley is the last one. I'm on the bus at this point, and Liam is sitting behind me, knowing I want to sit with Riley. She gets on and plops herself down.

She motions to the back of us at Liam. "Plan is in action then?" she asks quietly.

I nod, worried that she's upset.

"Just be careful, 'kay?"

I nod. "I will. I promise I won't fall in love any time soon."

We are the topic of conversation all day. Every class I go into, I get looks. The girls are all probably wondering how I bagged the most eligible guy—because let's be honest; we all want the bad boy—and all the guys look at me in a different light. Liam comes over at lunch and sits with us, sitting very close to me. Riley and her friend, Susan, roll their eyes at each other even though Susan doesn't know it isn't real. I start getting used to the attention and let it roll off me. By the end of the first day, I'm kind of liking it, liking that everyone thinks I'm with Liam.

Chapter Six

Liam

"So, you're not gonna tell me where we're going?" I ask Rosie.

She gives me a smug grin. "Nope, but I know you will like it."

"You are driving me crazy." I say it as though I'm exasperated, but I'm not. Truth is I think she's the only person who has ever organised a surprise for me, and yeah, I know how sad that sounds. But unfortunately, it's true. I smile as I remember her bounding over to me yesterday, excitement evident on her face. She wanted to take me somewhere today—Saturday—as a surprise, but we have to get the train. I have no idea where we're going, but I love that she's so excited; it's contagious.

We are just arriving at the train station, and I see her checking the notice board. I look up. We could be going anywhere.

She looks so cute, frowning away, trying to concentrate. She is so intelligent, but then, little things that I find easy she sometimes struggles with. She can be ditzy, and I love that about her. Well, not love, obviously, but she's cool. Really cool.

She looks over at me doubtfully. "Okay. So, I'm still not telling you what we're doing, but I will tell you that we are going to Harrogate."

Wow. That's quite far. What could be in Harrogate?

"Oh-kay . . ."

"I *might* need you to help me get on the right platform." She smiles at me sheepishly, making me laugh.

On her phone, she pulls something up on her screen and then hands it to me. It's the Trainline app.

I study it for a moment. "Okay. So, we have to get the Manchester to Leeds train. Then, the Leeds to Harrogate train. Manchester to Leeds leaves in 10 minutes, according to this, from platform 4." I look up and see the way to platform four. I grab her hand. "Come on." I hand her the phone back with the tickets pulled up, enjoying how her hand feels in mine and trying not to notice that it fits perfectly.

"You're laughing at me on the inside, aren't you?"

I chuckle. "I'm not; I promise. I might laugh at you on the outside to your face, but I promise I won't hide it."

"Ha-ha. Geography is not my strong point."

"This isn't geography, babe. This is just following instructions."

"Shut up," she says and shoves me with her shoulder.

"How confident are you that you can get to our destination once we get to Harrogate?"

She grins. "Ah, well, that's where we don't need to worry. We're just getting a taxi to our destination."

"And, that would be...?" I'm just trying my luck, attempting to get info.

"I'm not telling you! Stop asking." She looks like she's thinking for a moment. "You know, this is going to be so embarrassing if you think this surprise is crap."

"I already love it, seeing as it's the first one anyone has ever planned for me."

She frowns. "You're kidding, right?"

I shrug. "Afraid not. So, you see, it's good already."

I don't want her to feel sorry for me. I probably shouldn't have told her that. That's the problem with Rosie; she's so easy to be around that, sometimes, I forget myself, relax too much and blurt anything out.

"I'm sorry, Liam." Her voice is soft.

I shake my head. "Don't feel sorry for me, Rosie. I don't need that."

She looks down. "I know you don't, but I'm still sorry."

"Thanks." I give her a lopsided grin.

When we get to the platform, we see the train is already in, so we get on and take a seat. I'm excited that I get to spend all day with her when I'd just be stuck in at home usually. Maybe I'd go and hang out with friends, maybe go for a run, but my weekends are long and boring. At least this will make it go quicker.

We get comfortable. A couple of minutes later, the whistle goes, and the train sets off.

I see her fiddling in her bag, and then, she produces two cans of Pepsi and two bags of crisps. She looks so proud of herself.

"Aw, you brought snacks. How good are you?"

She grins. "I know, right? So, this train is an hour, and the next one is only 20 minutes?"

I nod. "Yeah. Gimme, gimme!" I ask her to hand over the goodies, and once I've had a drink of my Pepsi, I set it on the table. "Your mum and dad okay with you doing this today?" I ask her.

Her mum is a real piece of work from what she's told me, always running her down as if she didn't have enough of that at her old school. But her dad and brother are cool; I've met them a couple of times. I met her mum, too, and she was fine, I guess. But I didn't talk to her for long.

"Yeah, they were fine. They thought it was a good idea when I told them what I was planning. Well, Dad did. Mum just went on and on about what I should wear that would be most flattering in order to hide my bum."

"If you hid that bum of yours, it would make me really mad. That's one of my favourite things to look at."

She gasps and goes red. "Liam, you can't say that!"

"Just speaking the truth." And, that is the truth. I have to force my eyes away when she has her fitted jeans on and a short top. There ain't nothing wrong with her bottom; no way. The fact that her mum tells her there is just makes my blood boil.

She grins to herself. Maybe, if I keep saying nice things to her, she will actually believe them.

I lean back, "So, we've been together for two weeks now. Everyone well and truly believes we're together. How do you think it's going?"

She glances at me. "Yeah . . . Good. I mean, everyone at school believes it, I think. I guess the test will come at Connor's next party."

"Yeah. I've been thinking about that. We will probably have to make out soon, you know." I *do not* hate that idea.

I see her swallow. "Yeah . . . Probably."

She takes a deep breath. "Anyway, yeah. It's good. People are talking to me that never would have, I think, and all your friends are nice to me. Some of the girls are, too; I like Harper and her friends. I feel like I'm settling into school a lot better than I would have if you hadn't had your idea. What about you?"

"Yeah. All good with me. All my work is looking good, and teachers have commented that I seem to have calmed down. Some have mentioned you, saying that you are a good influence on me."

"That's good. When do you think we should end it?"

Does it sound like there is sadness in her voice?

55

"Um, not yet. I think maybe after the New Year. We could keep it going 'til then. That's not long off. By then, all the teachers will definitely know that I mean business with my work, and with you helping me with any work I'm stuck on, they will have noticed an improvement in my work by then, too." I hope it doesn't sound like I'm trying too hard, but I don't want this to end yet.

"Yeah. That's a good idea. We will keep it going until after Christmas." She drums her fingers on her chin as though in thought. "Hmmm . . . What Christmas gift should I ask for?" She grins at me, laughing.

I know she's joking, but I'm going to get her something. I mean, she's doing this for me today. At the very least, at the end of all this, I'll hopefully be left with a really good friend. I mean, I don't want anything more. I don't do relationships, but she is way cool. I could definitely keep her in my life. Trouble is . . . I fancy her. I'm trying not to, but those eyes, that hair, and that bloody mouth of hers . . . I love her laugh, too. Yeah. It's a problem, finding her attractive, but I'm just going to have to push it to the back of my mind.

We chat for the rest of the journey about this and that, and our exchange at Leeds goes fine. The journey is short to Harrogate, so we are soon pulling into the station. I've never been to Harrogate, and neither has she. So, it's a new adventure for both of us.

We get into a cab at the station where Rosie hands the taxi driver a piece of paper.

"Please can you take us to this address? It's a surprise. He doesn't know where I'm taking him," she asks the driver.

The taxi driver grins at her. "Sure thing, honey. No problem."

She sits back and grins at me. She is *loving* this. I've been wracking my brains, trying to figure out where I'm going, but I have no clue.

After a short while, the taxi pulls up in front of a large building, she pays him, and we get out. We go over to the building where I spot a plaque on the wall.

Museum of woodwork and handcrafted wood

My stomach plummets through to the floor. She's brought me all this way to a wood museum. She knows I love woodwork, that I want to do it for a career, and she found this place and brought me all this way. I don't believe someone would do something so lovely for me. I look at her, dumbfounded.

"You-you brought me to a woodwork museum?"

She nods, looking shy. "Well, yeah. You love all the carving stuff, right? You won't believe this, but this place was on the news the other day when Dad was watching it. A piece of woodwork had raised loads of money for charity, and when I saw it, I thought, 'Oh my God! How much would you love it?' You can see all the different ways of carving, and they even do demos, which I know you'll think are a bit lame because you can do it yourself. But still, I thought it might be fun?"

I'm still speechless. I can't believe she's done this. This is, without a doubt, the nicest thing anyone has *ever* done for me in my whole life.

"I don't know what to say, Rosie... I--"

Her face falls. "You don't want to go in?"

I nod. "Are you crazy? Of course, I do! I just can't believe you've brought me here."

She looks relieved. "God, don't do that to me. I thought I'd messed up, then."

I lean in and kiss her on the cheek, her skin feeling so soft and smooth against my lips, and the scent of her... She has perfume on, and she smells so good, that scent mixed with hair conditioner or something. Perfection.

She looks up at me, her eyes wide.

"Thank you," I whisper.

She gives me a soft smile while sliding her arm in mine to link us. "Come on; let's go in."

The museum is fantastic. *She* is fantastic. We have a great time and such fun. There are so many things I'm interested in; I'm like a kid in a toy shop. Then, when she finally drags me out, I take her to a café for lunch, my treat, to say thank you. After that, we head back on the train.

When we get home, it's late. I hold her hand, walking up the path to her house, stalling because the last thing I want to do right now is leave her and go home. *Please ask me in; please ask me in.* I don't want today to be over.

We both bought a keyring from the museum, our initials made of wood, and I finger it in my pocket as we reach her door.

"Rosie, I can't tell you how much I loved today. You are the best."

She smiles. "I'm glad you liked it. It was fun, wasn't it?"

I look down at her, her eyes bright, sparkling, full of life. God, I want to kiss her. *Should I kiss her?* I look down at her mouth, those gorgeous, plump lips. Then, I look back up at her eyes.

I can't help it; I need to kiss her. I put my hand on her hip and lean my head in, standing so close to her that I can feel her breathing. She sees what I'm doing, and she doesn't object. In fact, her breathing is picking up with anticipation. She *wants* me to kiss her.

I need her permission for this. "Rosie . . ." My mouth is so close to hers that I feel her exhale.

The front door swings open, and her mum is standing there.

57

"Oh, Rosie! I thought I heard something."

Damn. *Damn.* I so wanted to kiss her then. That couldn't have been worse timing.

"Oh, hi, Mum. Yeah. Just me. Just saying 'bye' to Liam."

The only thing that cheers me up is that she sounds disappointed, too.

Her mum looks at me through narrowed eyes. "Oh, okay. Bye, Liam. Hope you've had a good day and enjoyed your surprise."

"Yeah. It was great, Mrs. Wilcock. I had the best day."

Her mum doesn't move. She stays there and, obviously, isn't going any-where.

Rosie turns to me and rolls her eyes. "Okay. I'll see you Monday?"

I nod, "Yeah. Bye, Rosie. Thanks again."

I turn around and walk down her path, sad that I'm going home, but at least her mum interrupting stopped me from kissing her. What was I thinking? Do I want to complicate things? She's going to think I want an actual girlfriend if I do things like that. No, that was for the best. Carry on as we were.

Chapter Seven

Rosie

"**F**ight! Fight! Everyone, there's a fight in the year 11 yard," a boy shouts as he runs past us to watch.

As usual, this starts a tsunami of students running towards the year 11 yard. Every time there is a fight, it amazes me that people just run to watch. Who cares? If two people want to beat the crap out of each other, then that's their stupid decision.

"Who is it?" another voice asks.

"Liam and Tommy," someone else shouts as they're running.

I look at Riley. It's Friday lunch; Liam was due to meet us here. "Liam is in a fight?"

Fear grips me. Why is he in a fight? He's been doing so well lately, really keeping his nose clean. "Come on, Riles; I need to go and check."

We both rush to the spot where everyone else is, but I can't get near. I can't see anything. I panic. Sod it! I barge my way through; I need to see what's going on.

My heart stops when I get to the front of the crowd. It *is* Liam. What is he doing? He has lost it. I can tell. He has a cut on his head, and his blazer is torn. The other guy, Tommy, who I've seen around but don't know him that well, has got a bloody nose. I can't let him carry on.

"Liam!" I shout. People around me turn to look at me. "Stop!"

He looks my way and gets thumped as he does. Oh, no. I distracted him!

Where are the teachers?

I don't want him to get hurt . . . God, I don't want him to fight! This is the opposite of how he should be acting. He's going to get suspended if they catch him. I need to end this now!

I move forward and throw myself in between them. Turning to Liam and pressing my hands against his chest, forcing him to step away from Tommy, I cry, "Stop, Liam. Please. Look at me."

He doesn't take any notice. He just pushes my arms off him and goes to get past me.

I grab him by the arm. "Liam, *please*. Look at me."

I don't recognise the guy that looks back at me. He's lost it.

I pull on his arm. "Please come with me. You're going to get in trouble."

"He shouldn't shout his mouth off about something he knows nothing about!"

"I don't know what he said, but what does it matter?"

"Talking crap about me, about my parents. What does he know?"

My heart sinks. This is something that has been bothering me. His parents, the lack of care they give him. Then, last night, his mum didn't show up for parents' evening. He said to me that it was no big deal, but I've gotten to know him a lot more in this past week. I can tell that it bothered him. She's never home. He is practically living alone.

"Please, Liam. Come with me. We'll get you cleaned up."

Tommy is breathing heavily, watching us. He wipes the blood away from his nose and then spits on the floor. Why do guys think it's cool to do that? Gross.

Liam looks down at me, and his shoulders droop. I put my hand on his waist, relieved I've gotten through to him.

"Come on." I reach down for his hand and grab hold, uncurling the fist. I try and think of where to go. Somewhere quiet where I can clean him up and talk to him. The tech lab. Liam has a key for it; Sir gave him one as he goes in so much. We really shouldn't use it for this, but it's an emergency. He lets me pull him away, push our way through the crowd. Some of the kids close in on Tommy, and I hear them asking what it was about. *Keep your mouth shut, Tommy, or you'll rile him up again.*

We walk to the tech lab in silence. When we get there, I let go of his hand and hold my hand out to him. He understands what I'm asking and roots around in his pocket for the key. I unlock the door and walk in.

"Sit," I order him. He sits on a chair away from the door so that no one can see us if they look inside.

I have a pack of tissues in my bag and my water bottle. That will have to do. I pour some water on the tissues. He's silent, watching me. I carefully dab the cut above his eye and look down at him. "What was that, Liam?"

He looks away from my gaze. "Nothing. He was just saying crap about my parents, that's all, telling me that I was an orphan, that I don't actually have parents, that I'm lying... The usual stuff."

"Oh, Liam. Why did you let him get to you?" I continue to dab the blood away, and once I've got most of it, I pat it dry. Luckily, it was only a small cut. It just looked worse because of the blood. I can hardly see it now; no doubt it will swell a little, though.

"I don't know. He annoyed me so much I couldn't seem to control myself. I lost it."

He's hurting; I can tell. And, I don't mean physically. How he feels about his parents is bad enough, but now, he knows other people have noticed, too.

"Why can't she just make an effort, just one time?" His voice breaks, and he clears his throat.

"I'm sorry, Liam. Have you tried talking to her?"

"What? Guilt her into spending time with me, actually being a mother? No thanks. I shouldn't have to, should I?"

I shake my head, "No, you shouldn't, Liam, but maybe she needs to you to tell her that she's not much of a mother right now. Maybe it needs to be said. You shouldn't be on your own as much as you are."

"It's a great idea, but it wouldn't do any good. I'm on my own, and that's just the way it is."

I give him a small smile. "Well, in some strange, weird way, you have me now, too, for however long that is."

He grabs hold of my hand, the one patting his eye dry and squeezes it. "Yeah. I do. Thank you." His voice is gravelly, full of emotion. It chokes me up.

"You're welcome," I whisper.

"Come on. Let's get out of here before we get caught. You can hardly see the cut now that I've cleaned it up. You are going to get a black eye, I think, but it's not come out yet. You really could do with some ice or something on it."

"I'm good. Come on." He stands up.

I turn to him. "Wanna hang out tonight?"

He smirks. "Why? You feel sorry for me?"

I bat him on the arm. "Don't be stupid; we've been hanging out nearly every night, Liam. How is tonight any different?"

He shrugs. "I guess."

"Why don't you get the bus home with me? We'll have dinner, take Sky for a walk, then just watch a movie or something."

"You're not gonna make me watch a chick flick, are you?"

"Depends. If Russ is in, I'm gonna be outnumbered, aren't I?"

He laughs. "I guess so." As I walk away in front of him, he pulls my hand back. "Thanks, Rosie. *Really* . . . Thanks."

He's so sincere, and my heartbeat speeds up. "It's okay. Meet me at the bus stop after school?"

He nods, lifts my hand, and kisses it. When his lips touch my skin, electricity shoots through me. His lips feel so soft on my skin. I can't help but think about what those lips would feel like on mine or on my neck. A tremor goes through me. It would be nice . . . So nice, but oh, so dangerous.

I pull him towards the door, and we leave the classroom, locking it behind us.

*****

When we get to my house, it's just my dad that's home. Mum is going to some Zumba evening straight from work, thankfully. He won't get to see how she can be with me. Russ must still be at college.

As soon as I open the door, Sky comes running towards me, my favourite part of the day by far. We rescued Sky about three years ago; she was around two then, they thought. It was right at the time when the trouble started at school, actually, when the mean girls began to notice me and wanted to use me as their next chew toy. Sky saved me on more than one occasion. Coming home to her when I felt all alone in the world, her being so happy to see me, she stopped me from going over the edge. It was pretty bad just before I left, and I was going into depression. But Sky was my guardian angel sent in dog form. She got to hear all my problems. She was my therapist. And, it's like she knew when I was upset. If I were crying in my room, she'd find me every single time and come and lie on the bed with her head on my lap. She's just the best thing in the world.

Liam bends down, and Sky comes over to him. She's met him a few times now, and she loves him. He always makes a fuss over her. The first time he saw her, he looked petrified, but he soon realised that, for her size, she's not much of a guard dog; she's the biggest pushover ever. He looked at me that first time for direction and asked, "Will she be okay with me?"

I laughed. "She's the biggest softy ever." I stood and motioned for him to come to her.

"Hey, girl," he said in the quietest, softest voice that made my heart melt.

"Don't be nervous. They can tell when you're nervous, and they'll think you're the next thing for dinner."

His eyes went wide. It was cruel to tease him, but it was hilarious. I'd never seen anything remotely like fear in him before.

I linked his arm and pulled him near to me. "I'm kidding. She is the softest dog you will ever meet. I promise."

He knelt, and Sky walked over to him tentatively, giving him a sniff. Then, her tail started to wag.

"See, you've got the tail wag. She likes you."

He exhaled. "Thank you, Lord." He reached up to scratch behind her ears which is her favourite thing in the world. That's all it took; he'd won her over. It seemed he had this effect on all the ladies, even of the canine variety.

So, that was the first time he'd met her. Now, they're like old friends. It doesn't take long for Sky, and she's only known him just over a week. She is either easy to please, or his natural charm has won her over. A bit of both, I think.

I kneel so that I can give her the hello she deserves. "Come here, girl. How was my girl's day? You're so good. Yes, you are." Her tail is wagging at me like crazy as she tries to kiss me. It's a reunion. Seven hours to her must feel like a lifetime.

I look up to find him grinning at me. "You know, you are way nicer to her than you are to any human."

I smile at him. "I'm nice to you. What do you mean?" I'm teasing him because I know it's true; she's my favourite thing in the whole world.

"Yeah. You are, but you take it to a whole new level with her. I'd like to be in her shoes once in a while."

"Aw, you want me to tickle your ears?" I stand, laughing.

He steps in closer to me and puts his hand on my waist. "I'll give it a go if it's an offer."

The air goes thick suddenly, the atmosphere pressing down on me. I'm so conscious of his hand on my waist and how it feels. His touch makes me feel unsure and confident all at the same time. We look at each other, and neither of us speaks. I could drown in these eyes, the colour like nothing I've ever seen before, and they look brighter right now.

"I think you only benefit from that if you're a dog."

"Oh, I don't know..." He tips his head to the side as though thinking.

I laugh and step away from him, and his arm falls back to his side. He's flirting. That *was* flirting, right? I mean I've never experienced it before, but he was definitely being playful.

We say hello to dad who is doing something in the garage. He works from home a lot so is often here when I get home from school.

"Dad, Liam has come home with me. He's gonna have dinner with us. Is that okay?" I ask him. I know it will be. He knows Liam is on his own a lot at home.

He looks over at us. "Sure. That's fine. Hey, Liam. How's it going?"

Liam nods. "Hey, Mr. Wilcock. . . Yeah. All good."

My dad frowns and points to his head. "You get into a little trouble there?"

Oh, God. I'd forgotten about his head. He had to throw his jacket away. It had been torn beyond repair. *Thank goodness Dad didn't see that.*

Liam glances at me quickly then nods at my dad. "Yeah, sir. I'm afraid I did. Someone was saying something bad about my family, and I'm afraid I lost my temper. I'm working on it."

I'm shocked that he's just come out and told the truth to my dad. I don't know what I expected but definitely not that. I admire him for being so honest. My dad will appreciate his honesty; I know he will.

Dad nods. "Ah, right. I like that you stick up for your family, son, but yes. You need to try and control your temper if you are to get ahead in life. You should do Jujitsu like our Russ. It's a great way to get your anger and stresses out."

Liam tips his head to one side. "You know, I'd never thought about it, but that's a good idea. I'll give it some thought; maybe, if I can fit it in around basketball, I might give it a go."

Dad gives him a genuine smile. "Great. Let me know if you decide to go ahead. You can have a chat with Russ about it."

He nods at Dad, and then, I usher him out of the garage. "See you later, Dad."

"Sure, honey."

I turn to Liam once we're back inside the house. "That was cool, you being honest with my dad like that."

He shrugs. "No point lying. Anyone can tell I've been in a fight."

I nod. "Want to do the dog walk or tea first? Are you hungry?"

He nods. "I'm starving. I'm always hungry. I had a big lunch at school, but yeah. I could eat."

I nod and look in the fridge. Mum batch cooks and leaves the food in there. "Okay. So, there is beef stew or chicken fajita casserole."

His eyes light up. I bet he doesn't get meals cooked for him at home. "Beef stew, please."

I nod and put it in the microwave then tell him I'm going to get changed. I leave Liam in the kitchen with Sky.

When I get back downstairs in my yoga pants and t-shirt, I see Liam's eyes go over my outfit. He knows I caught him doing it as he smiles to himself and looks down at his feet. Does he like what he sees? Is that possible? It kind of looked like he did, but that doesn't make any sense. I'm the opposite of any girl he would ever go for, I'm sure.

Dad walks in. "What's cooking?"

"Beef casserole. There's lots, enough for all of us. Do you want some?"

He shakes his head. "No, I promised Russ Chinese tonight. Man United are playing Chelsea."

Liam speaks up. "Oh, yeah. It's going to be a good match."

"You're welcome to join us, son." *Bless my dad.*

Liam glances over at me, looking hopeful. My heart hurts for him. When does he get to hang out with his dad and watch football? Never. I need to give him this.

"Yeah, you can watch it. I'm not a big fan, but I can watch it, too." I lean into Liam. "I should warn you, though. They're Chelsea supporters." My grandad is from London way, so Dad grew up as a Chelsea supporter.

"Oh, yeah. It's okay. I'm a city fan, so no fights will break out. We'll be fine." He laughs.

"Brilliant! See you later then, Liam." Dad goes back into his office in the garage.

Liam and I eat our beef stew with crusty bread. Liam enjoys it as though he's never eaten a meal before. Once we've eaten, we get Sky ready to go for a walk. I decide to go to the park and through the woods. Usually, I wouldn't go there on my own, even though Sky can be quite the protector. It's not worth the risk, so I always stick to the roads. I don't need to tonight, however. I feel bad that Liam is still in his uniform, so I suggest walking around to his house to get changed. Then, we can carry on to the woods. Plus, it's freezing; he will need to get a jacket, seeing as his school jacket went in the bin.

When we walk up to Liam's house, it's all shrouded in darkness. It's 6.30, so it's still early. As lovely as the house is—and big—it looks so cold and uninviting.

He turns to me sadly. "Shocker. No one is home. Come on in. I'll just be a minute."

I go into the living room. He assures me it's okay with Sky; it's not like anyone will know anyway. I look around the living room. What must it be like living here? He must be so lonely. Is this why he gets in trouble at school? Is he wanting attention? He must feel like no one cares if he's living or not. My mum is a nightmare, but at least she's present. And, I love dad and Russ to bits. I just don't know how I'd cope if I had to live like this, not having anyone to come home to when you've had a crappy day. I feel so sad.

I push my feelings to the back of my mind when I hear Liam coming down the stairs. The last thing I want him to see is pity.

He gives me such a genuine smile. "Ready."

We head out of the house and down the lane towards the park. It's not a long walk. When we get to the park, we walk through and head towards the path to the woods. It's dark now, but there are little lights every so often down the footpath. The volunteers of the park have put fairy lights in some of the trees in the woods. It's lovely and helps us to see where we're going. I reach down to let Sky off the lead, and she goes bounding off; she never goes far.

"So, I've been thinking . . ." Liam suddenly says.

"Okay. That sounds scary. What about?" *Has he decided that he doesn't want to do this fake relationship thing anymore?* It's going so well, apart from the fight today, but he hasn't got in trouble for that yet, up to now, anyway.

"Us . . . Being in this relationship." He holds his fingers to make air quotes when he says "relationship." My heart sinks. He's going to put an end to it.

"What about it? You dumping me already?" I try to make a joke of it when inside, my heart is beating a hundred miles an hour.

"What? No! I was thinking about this party on Saturday. I mean we can get away with only a certain amount of affection and PDA at school, but at the party, people are gonna expect to see certain things, me and you doing certain things."

"I get that they're gonna want to see us together, but what do you mean?"

"Well, I think they're gonna expect us to kiss." He looks a little nervous.

My stomach plummets through to my toes. Is he serious?

"Well, they're gonna be disappointed then, aren't they?" I know that there's no way on Earth he'd want to kiss me, even if it is fake.

"The thing is that they're never going to believe we're seeing each other if we don't step it up on the PDA. Is it so bad to kiss me?"

He's joking, right?

I give a nervous laugh. "No . . . No. Definitely not bad . . ."

"So, what's the problem?"

"You want me to kiss you on Saturday night?" I ask. My voice sounds shaky.

"No. *I* want to kiss *you*."

I swallow. God, this is mortifying. How do I tell him I've never kissed anyone before? How did I get myself in this situation?

"I don't know. I-I'm not sure."

"Come on. It's not like we're getting married or anything. It's just a kiss."

"That might be all it is for you. You kiss girls all the time. It's a bit of a bigger deal for me."

"Why? It's just a bit of fun, Rosie."

"You think it would be fun to kiss me?" Am I putting words into his mouth?

"Yeah. I mean, I guess. It's all for a good cause, right?" He rubs the back of his neck, a sign that he's getting stressed.

Just get it over with, Rosie.

"I've never kissed anyone before," I blurt out.

He stops in his tracks and grabs my arm, grounding me to a halt. "Wait, what? *Are you serious?*"

I shrug, moving around some dirt with the toe of my boot, not being able to look directly at him right now. "We've not all got lots of experience, you know."

"How has someone like you never been kissed before?"

I look up at him. "Someone like me?"

"Well, yeah. Hot . . . Sexy."

I snort, just to prove how wrong he was about the sexy part. "Yeah. Right."

"I mean it."

I shrug his arm off gently and carry on walking, "I haven't had any experience with boys. The girls at my last school made my life so miserable, and they were pretty popular. So, even if a boy *did* want to talk to me—which I seriously doubt—there's no way they would approach me. Their life would have been made a living hell."

"Have I told you how much I really hate the girls from your last school?"

I laugh. "Not as much as me."

"I'm sorry you had such a rough time," he says quietly.

"Thanks. I'm just glad it's over."

"So, what do you think we should do about the kiss then? Do you want to kiss me now?"

I stop in my tracks. Sky is close by, sniffing around. "What? Here?"

"If we kiss now, then on Saturday, you wouldn't be so nervous, and you'd look like a pro."

Wow, has it suddenly gotten really hot? Because I feel like I'm sweating all over. So, my crush is suggesting kissing him here, in the woods, at night, with fairy lights in the trees above us. Is this real? Well, actually, no; it's not. It's all to keep up our fake relationship. But I can pretend, just for five minutes, that it is real.

"I-I guess we could." I feel the butterflies flying around my stomach, trying to make their way out.

He grabs my hand and pulls me over to the trunk of a big horse-chestnut tree. He turns me around so that my back is against the trunk.

He looks down at me but doesn't say anything for a while; he just looks at me. Then, I feel one of his hands go on my waist, under my open jacket. I can feel the heat of his hand practically scorching my skin through my coat. Oh, God. This is happening. He steps in closer to me, and I take a sharp breath in. "Relax, Rosie."

I'm trying to; I really am. My whole body is tense.

"Put your hand around my neck." I do as he says and slide my hand up around his neck, touching the skin there and the bottom of his hairline. My hand is cold, and his neck his warm, lovely and warm.

His eyes crinkle in the corners when he smiles at me. I could get lost in these eyes. Who am I kidding? I am lost.

I feel his head dip towards me. *This is it.*

Just as he's about to touch his mouth to mine, he mutters, "Ready?"

I give a little nod. Then, I feel his mouth on me.

It's soft but firm, his lips moving over mine in a way that makes me feel like I'm drowning—in a good way. I'm drowning in him. I feel his other hand cup my face as a noise escapes him that sounds like a growl as he deepens the kiss. I like that sound. Our mouths move together as though our lips were made for each other. He steps closer so that his body is flush with mine, and I feel him grab onto my waist. I wind my other arm around his neck as I fall further and further into a Liam fog, pulling him into me, getting lost in this kiss. I think I've found my most perfect thing to do. Ever. I want to kiss him forever. He doesn't seem to be wanting to end it any time soon, either. He breaks off from my mouth and bites my lower lip. Mmm, I like that, and a little moan escapes me. He moves his head down, kissing a trail down my jawline then down my neck, all the while my fingers touching the hair at the bottom of his neck, my breathing rapid.

I feel his hot breath at my ear when he says, "You honestly haven't done this before, Rosie?"

"No." My voice sounds hoarse. His mouth finds mine again. We kiss and kiss. I feel his chest pressed against mine and can clearly feel his heart beating rapidly. He breaks off and looks into my eyes, breathing as though the kiss affected him as much as it affected me.

"I can't believe you've never done that before."

"I promise you're my first."

His eyes flash. "I like that I'm your first. At least you got shown how it should be done properly for your first experience." He grins.

I bat his shoulder, relieved that the tension between us has eased. "That was . . .fun." It was more than fun. It was amazing, life-changing, out of this world. But I can't say that.

"Yeah . . . Fun," he says, but he doesn't say it like he believes it. Was he thinking it felt more than fun, like I was thinking? Who knows?

I push myself off the tree trunk, not wanting to break the spell between us but knowing I needed to. "Come on. Let's keep walking. Five more minutes, and then, we're back to where we started and can head back. We need you to be back for the football game."

All through the football match, all I can think of is that kiss, how it felt. I can still feel his lips on mine. Surely all kisses do not feel as good as that. He can kiss. Exactly how much experience does he have? A lot, I'm guessing. I know that I should be looking forward to Saturday just so that I get to do it again, feel his lips on mine again, but this is only going to end in me getting hurt; I know it. But as I watch him, settled down in my living room, watching football with my dad and brother instead of home alone in an empty house, I can't help but think how much I like him being here.

Chapter Eight

Rosie

I'm in the library, my favourite, go-to place, just reading my notes on history to see if I've missed anything in my homework. It's Thursday lunch. Riley has a gym competition so has gone to another school with the gym team. Her friends—the ones that I usually hang with—are on it, too, so I'm friendless today. I thought about going to Liam at the workshop, knowing he'll probably be there, but that's his downtime, where he releases his stress. So, I decide to leave him be and hang out in the library. We're spending so much time together. People are starting to comment that we're inseparable, and I'm getting way too comfortable with it. What am I going to do when this is all over? I need to spend some time on my own. I can't stop thinking about that kiss. I felt surrounded by him, protected. It was the most fantastic thing I've ever felt, and I felt it in every nerve ending of my body. The way his mouth felt against mine, the taste of him. God, I could lose myself in this guy if I'm not careful.

I get up to go down one of the aisles, looking for another book on the American civil war just to make my notes a little beefier. That's when I hear them.

"Yeah, and Kelsie told me that he's taking her to Connor's again on Saturday night."

"Are you *serious?*"

"So I've heard."

"This is so unlike Liam. I don't get it."

I freeze when I hear Liam's name. They don't know I'm here. I don't recognise the voices.

"What does he see in her anyway? She's a beast."

My heart sinks. I *really* hate mean girls.

"I know, right? There's no way he can be taking her because he likes her. He must feel sorry for her or something."

I try to get a sneaky look at who's talking. One is Chelsea, the girl he was kissing the first Saturday before all this started. I don't know who the other one is.

"Well, don't forget he made out with you when he was with her, so he can't be that into her."

"I know, and she interrupted, the cow. He said that he was just helping her settle into Arrowsmith. Why is he the good Samaritan all of a sudden? And, did you hear what he did to Mark when he said something about her?" Chelsea asks.

I go cold. What is she talking about?

"Yeah, apparently he pinned him up against the wall when he said something. That was right at the beginning, too."

I don't know anything about this. He didn't mention anything to me. I try and cast my mind back to think when it could have been, but I'm drawing a blank. He's been defending me?

"Mark's his teammate, too. There must be something in it for him. They've been spending a lot of time together."

"Yeah. Maybe he actually likes her?" Chelsea sounds sad.

"Are you crazy? Why would he be into her when he could have you. There is an explanation. I'm sure of it. And, have you ever seen them kiss? I've never seen anything physical between them. There is something fishy, I'm telling you."

Chelsea sighs. "I hope so, but I can't help thinking that he might be into her."

"Look, we'll make sure you look amazing on Saturday night. He'll fall at your feet."

She giggles, and they go off to get whatever book they came in for.

I need to sneak out without them seeing me. I take a picture with my phone of the pages I need in my book, and then, when I know the coast is clear, I grab my bag from the table and get out of there as fast as I can. So much for blending in and staying out of trouble. This Liam thing is having the opposite effect. I thought it would help, but it's making me enemies. I hate school. The sad thing is, I actually love school, love the work. Sometimes, I feel like I can't get enough of the learning, and yes, I know that makes me a dork. But I do love it. I just hate all the rubbish that comes with it, the meanness. Why can't people just be nice? I get knots in my stomach as a familiar feeling starts to build. Panic. I'm panicking that things are going to go downhill here when they were going so well. I need to go to Liam and tell him it's all off, that we can't carry on with our arrangement anymore. And, what the hell was that about? Him nearly fighting with one of his teammates about me? Why didn't he tell me? I know why. Because whoever it was would have been saying mean things about me. It's sweet he defended me, but he wouldn't need to if we weren't doing this in the first place. We need to end it now.

I know he'll be in the tech lab, working on his current project, so I head over there. I look through the door; he's there, head bent down, really working on something. He's concentrating so much that he doesn't hear me open the door.

"Hey." I startle him, and he drops whatever he's doing.

"Hey!" he says grinning at me. "You scared me then! I was concentrating."

"Sorry. I just needed to talk to you."

He moves towards me, grabs my hand, and leads me to a seat. "What's up?"

"I don't think we should carry this on. It's not working out."

"What? Why? Is it because of last night? Because of what I said we'd have to do on Saturday? Because I kissed you?"

I shake my head. I don't want him to think it was because of the kiss; that was incredible. "No . . . It's just-I think it's doing me more harm than good. I don't want everyone to notice me, and everyone is at the moment because of you."

"You're crazy if you think that no one notices you, Rosie. You're gorgeous, you ace every class, and you're nice to everyone. It doesn't matter if you're with me or not; people notice you."

"Yeah, but they might not hate me. They hate me right now because I'm with you."

"Has someone said something to you?" He looks so concerned.

I shake my head. "No, but I get the impression that there are other girls here who think they have a claim on you."

He looks mad. "Right. Tell me what's happened now so that I can sort this out. What is it with girls? Who the hell do they think they are? If someone thinks they have a claim on me, they couldn't be more wrong. Who was it?"

I tilt my head at him. He couldn't be this naive, could he? I'm supposed to be the naive one. "Who do you think?"

He stares at me for a moment, those blue eyes really thinking. "Not Chelsea?"

"Yes, Chelsea. I was in the library. I overheard her talking to her friend. She wasn't very nice; the things they were saying were pretty mean."

"I don't believe her. Is she for real? I have made it clear so many times that I'm not interested."

"You were kissing her the first time you took me to Connor's." I point out the obvious.

He sighs. "Yeah. That wasn't a good move, but would you believe me if I told you I did it for an easy life? She's always all over me, and she was doing it again that night. I couldn't be bothered with the confrontation of turning her down, so I just went along with it. I know how bad that sounds."

A guy's way out. Easy. "Yeah. I guess I get that. The thing is that they know that you took me to that party. So, they don't think there's anything romantic between us because you took me but kissed her."

"I'll talk to her, make her realise that nothing will ever happen between us and tell her to stop bitching about you."

"No! Don't do that. Don't mention me. I don't want you to talk about me."

He runs his hands over his hair. "I'm sorry, Rosie. I'll sort it. Please don't finish this thing. It's working so well for me. My maths teacher said he had noticed an improvement; he is impressed. Yesterday, my geography teacher asked me how I'd managed to get you to go out with me. She was joking, but I could tell she was impressed. I know you're probably thinking I'm getting a lot more out of this than you, but come with me Saturday and see how it goes. Please? See if you have a good time, and if you don't, we'll stage a breakup. Okay? I promise. I want you to feel good about coming to Arrowsmith after what you've been through. I don't want one girl to ruin it for you."

"One girl can do a lot of damage," I say quietly.

He shakes his head. "Not Chelsea. She doesn't have power. There isn't one girl like that here. There's a popular group, sure, and yeah. She's in it, but they don't rule the school."

"There's something else . . .Chelsea and her friend mentioned a problem between you and one of your teammates, said that you were defending me or something. What was that?"

He shakes his head. "That doesn't matter."

"Did you nearly get into a fight defending me?"

He stares at me but doesn't say anything; his silence speaks volumes.

"So, you did . . . I thought I was supposed to be keeping you out of trouble, not getting you into more?"

"It was before you and I even made our arrangement. I didn't like the way he was talking about you. He was disrespecting you, saying things about you that I didn't like. I would have stuck up for anyone that way. He needed to be put in his place."

Is that true? Or, was it because it was me? I suppose I'll never know. Part of me loves that he did that for me, loves that he came to my defence when no one else ever has.

I sigh. I feel so bad that things are going well for him with this arrangement, especially when I know things are so bad for him at home, and he's been nothing but nice to me. "Okay. Fine. I'll see how it goes Saturday."

He looks relieved. "When you came in here saying you wanted to break it off, I thought I must be a terrible kisser."

I burn up with embarrassment that he brought up the kiss. *Grow up, Rosie. Stop blushing.* I hate that I blush so easily. I give a nervous laugh. "No . . . Definitely not that."

He raises his eyebrows in a flirty way. "So, you liked it?"

"It was okay." I sigh dramatically so that he knows I'm joking.

He stands up, pulling me up to standing, and slides a hand around my waist. "Oh, really? Only okay?"

His face is so close to mine. "Well . . . Maybe more than okay."

"Want a do-over right now?" His voice is low and husky.

In here? Is he crazy? "What? No!"

He laughs. "I'm joking." He leans in and kisses my cheek. "Kind of . . . I'll save it for Saturday."

"You on the bus tonight?" I ask him.

He shakes his head. "No. I've got a game."

"A game tonight?"

"Yeah. It's here, straight after school."

Surely, as his girlfriend or whatever, I should go and watch. "Shouldn't I . . . Well, shouldn't I come and watch you?"

He raises his eyebrows. "You want to watch?"

I shrug. "It would be something I would do, don't you think? If we were seeing each other?"

"Well . . . Yeah, but I didn't want to ask. I figure you're doing enough for me. I didn't want to put this on you, too."

"No. It's fine. I don't mind. It might be fun." I shrug.

He looks so pleased that I said I would go; I'm happy that I offered. I bet no one ever goes to watch him. I bet girls turn up to ogle him, sure. But actually be there to support him? I bet that's new.

"Cool." He looks like he's thinking about something and then looks at his phone. "I have science next with Harper; she normally goes to the games. Edward plays. Want me to mention you're going? You can sit with her?"

I like Harper and her friends, contrary to what I thought when I first met them. They're genuinely lovely which just goes to show that I shouldn't judge a book by its cover. "Yeah. Sure. That would be good. Thanks. You look after me."

He looks up from his phone and grins at me, giving me a wink.

Wow. I feel like my legs are going to give way from under me.

"I do, don't I? See you at the game then. I'll throw you my vest when we win."

My eyes go wide. "Do you actually do that?"

"Well, with the horrified look on your face, I am definitely going to do it now!"

I laugh and hit him on the arm, wondering how he managed to cheer me up when I came in here so down. I leave him to it and go to my next class, excited for the game later and that I get to see him in action.

The end of the school day finally comes, and I make my way over to the gym. I've never watched a game of basketball before. I know this school team does well. Usually, a decent crowd stays behind to watch them. I saw Riley at breaktime and told her that I was going to the game, but she has practice tonight. Just as I'm walking into the entrance, I hear someone shout my name. I turn around, and Harper is there, waving. I go over to her. "Hi! Did Liam tell you to take pity on me and let me sit with you guys?"

She smiles. She is so pretty. "Yeah. Come and sit with us. We always get the really good seats just behind the players."

I nod and follow her. I say "hi" to the others and take a seat. Checking the clock, I see that we've only got 15 minutes to the game. I soak up the atmosphere. I could never come to things like this at my other school. Suddenly, a feeling of gratefulness overwhelms me. I wouldn't be here if it weren't for Liam. I am helping him, but he is helping me more than he realises.

The opposing team comes on the court and starts to warm up to a few cheers from the away supporters, and then, our team comes out to a massive cheer. I spot Liam a mile away and enjoy watching him from afar. I don't realise I have a smile on my face while I'm watching him until Harper says, "Wow. You have it bad."

I look at her. "What?"

"The look on your face when you saw him then? It says it all. Don't worry. From what I've seen, he has it just as bad for you."

"I don't know . . ."

"Trust me. I've seen the way he looks at you. I've never even known him to have a girlfriend before."

"It's going well . . . Really well." That's not a lie; that is the god's honest truth.

"Have you kissed him?"

I blush and look down at my hands, and she laughs. "So, that's a yes."

I hold up my index finger and thumb in a little motion. "Maybe a little."

She laughs. "I knew it."

"Is he a good kisser?"

Well, I don't have anything to compare it to, but I know that he was good. "Oh, yeah . . . He did just fine."

"Yeah. I've heard that about him. If he can't be good with all the practice he gets, then there's something wrong."

Great. Thanks for reminding me that he's kissed half the school.

"What about you? Do you have your eye on anyone on the basketball team?"

Now, it's her turn to blush. "Me? No . . . No way. Edward would kill anyone from the team if they tried to hit on me. He says they'd only treat me bad. He's just the best. He's always looking out for me."

Interesting. Why did she blush?

The game is so fast paced that I'm on the edge of my seat, bouncing up and down. The hall had an electric atmosphere. The goals or hoops—or whatever you call them—were happening all the time from both teams. Liam scored a few; he was amazing. Where he gets his energy from, I don't know. I was tired just watching him, watching all of them. He was so impressive. And, talk about working the crowd. He was flirting with the whole audience. I swear. Every time he scored, he gave the biggest grin and waved at all the supporters. When he was hot, he lifted the bottom of his vest up to wipe the sweat off his head, showing off his toned stomach. Oh, he knew what he was doing alright.

The final whistle goes. It's 26 to the away team and 28 to us. We win! Everyone cheers, and all the team hugs each other. It's so great. For once, I feel like I'm part of something. I feel like crying; I'm so happy. Liam breaks off from hugging one of his team and starts striding over towards me. He starts to lift his top over his head. *No . . .* He's not going to, is he? *Please don't embarrass me, Liam.* I'm going to be mortified. But yes, he peels his vest off, and by the time he gets to me, he's shirtless. I try not to look; I really do, but with that cocky grin of his plastered all over his face, I can't help but notice how toned he his, those muscular biceps and that stomach, so flat and abs so well defined, shining with sweat. Wow. My mouth goes dry, and my heart starts to beat at a rapid pace. He hands me the top, and I grab hold of it. But he doesn't let go. He pulls me towards him and then puts his hand on my neck, kissing me hard and fast on the lips in front of everyone.

He looks down at me. "You like the game?"

I nod numbly. He's being an outstanding actor, putting this on for the crowd.

"Good. You gonna wait for me, and we'll go home together?"

Again, I nod numbly. *Way to be impressive, Rosie.*

He laughs and gives me another quick kiss, then runs away. He turns back to me as he's running, pointing at his vest. "Don't lose that. I need it for the next game."

I look down at his vest, the one he's been sweating in for the last 40 minutes. It takes all the restraint I have not to sniff it. Gross, I know.

Harper and the girls leave, and I wait around outside for Liam to come out. Everyone filters out. I feel all happy inside. I know it's wrong, but I'm just loving this week. I'm having the best week I've ever had a school. *Ever.* Sure, I heard those girls being nasty in the library, but Liam helped make me feel better about that. He's right. It's just one girl. I can handle one girl. The pros of this fake relationship are well outweighing the cons. As long as that's what I remember it is. Fake. Fake for him, and it has to be fake for me unless I want Riley to fall out with me for good. It's so hard, though. I'm getting feelings for him. I know I am. He's nothing but sweet to me, attentive, and he listens to me when there is something wrong. Plus, he's so attractive. I mean, I know how superficial I sound, but he's really hot.

I hear the door and turn around with a smile on my face, thinking it might be him, but my heart sinks. It's the girl from the library, Chelsea. I didn't even know she was watching the game. She looks surprised when she sees me there, and then, something flashes in her eyes. She's with two other girls.

"Well, well... If it isn't my replacement."

Chapter Nine

Rosie

My stomach plummets down to my feet. I can't handle confrontation. It just brings everything back to me that I'm trying so hard to forget. She's already won this little round, whatever she is planning on doing, because I just don't have the guts to fight back.

I feel defeated, bracing to take whatever she's going to throw at me, and then suddenly, something comes over me. Am I going to let people like her rule me for the rest of my life? When am I going to learn? It's about time I stood up for myself.

I take a deep breath. "Is there a problem?"

"Yeah. There's a problem with you. What has gone wrong with Liam that he could be interested in you?"

The two other girls give a nervous giggle. They will feel like they have to go along with whatever she says. I've had enough experience with bullies and their hangers-on to know the drill.

I feel something bubbling inside me. Anger, confidence, I'm not sure what, but it's something I've never come across before.

I make my voice sound as confident as possible. "Aw, really? Because he said he'd lost his mind when he thought he was interested in you."

They all gasp as Chelsea walks towards me. I keep my gaze fixed on her. I *will not* back down. This is a turning point, and I know it is. I either let her get the better of me right now and dread coming to school tomorrow, or I stick up for myself and refuse to play the victim.

I pick the second option for the first time in my life.

Chelsea leans into me, her eyes narrowing. "What did you say?" she asks in a low, threatening voice.

"Well, he did say that, but then, he did say that you didn't give him much of a choice about it anyway, said that you wouldn't leave him alone."

"You bitch!" she spits out.

I shake my head. "No, Chelsea. That's you."

"You think you're different? You think that, because you've been out with him more than a couple of times and he gives you his basketball shirt, he's in love? Well, think again. It won't be long before he moves on to someone else, someone that doesn't have a fat arse."

"Well, when he does, I'll be sure to come to you for advice, because you know how it feels, right? To be dumped by Liam?"

"Who the hell do you think you are?"

"She's my girlfriend, that's who." Liam is standing in the doorway of the gym, and he does not look happy. He walks over to us. "I think it's about time you and I had a little chat, Chelsea. I was hoping to do it in private to save you from embarrassment but seeing as you are acting like an evil little witch, I guess we'll do it now."

The other two girls gasp. Chelsea, on the other hand, remains silent. I see a flash of fear in her eyes.

"You see, Chelsea, I was never really interested in you. But you were there, you know? Always turning up where I was, always messaging me even though I never gave you my number. I just thought I'd throw you a bone when there were no better options."

Jeez, he's being brutal.

"So, Rosie here, well, she is the polar opposite to you in every way. She cares about people and is nice. You might want to try it sometime. And, just so you know, I love her arse, and I won't be getting rid of it any time soon."

Oh my God. Did he just say that? I try not to grin and look down at my feet.

Chelsea huffs. "Yeah. That's not what you said to me the other week when you had your tongue in my mouth."

Liam shrugs. "I didn't think she'd give me a chance then, so I was just hedging my bets. But believe me when I tell you now that all bets are well and truly off the table. Feel free to block me on your phone, too. I'll be doing that to your number. Now, is there anything else you want to say to me or my girlfriend?"

I love hearing him call me his girlfriend. I'm in trouble here. My brain knows it's fake, but my heart is hoping, somehow, that it can be real.

Chelsea has gone bright red. I almost feel sorry for her, *almost*. I mean, she just fell for a guy, right? Still, she didn't need to be so evil to me.

She huffs and spins around to her friends. "Come on. I don't need to be here to watch Liam make the biggest mistake of his life." And, they walk off.

I exhale the breath that I didn't realise I'd been holding and look up at Liam. He still looks mad, scowling as he watches them walk away. Then, he looks down at me, and it's gone. There's only concern there. "You okay?"

I nod.

"I'm sorry about that, about her. I know . . . I know, after everything you've been through, that that must have been awful."

I smile. "You know, I thought it was going to be, but I stood up for myself. Did you hear me?"

He grinned. "I did. You were awesome, actually. I didn't recognise you. You've found your courage from somewhere then?"

I link arms with him, and we start to walk towards the entrance of the school where Liam's ride, and mine, will be. "Apparently, I have. I think I might have you to thank for that."

"Well, as much as I'd love to take credit for that, that was all you. You were brilliant."

"I never thought I'd be able to stick up for myself like that. It was like something snapped in me. I thought I could either take it and have my last school experience all over again, or I could try something new. I liked the new thing!" I laugh.

"This needs a celebration. What are you doing now?"

I cringe. "I should be doing homework. No. *We* should be doing homework."

He leans in. "Let's sack it off and celebrate this new you."

"I can't. I've got too much homework, honestly, and I will break out in a cold sweat if I don't get it done."

He chuckles. "One step at a time then."

He drops me off at home, and we say our goodnights.

Nothing can spoil my mood tonight, not even Mum greeting me as soon as I got home. "Rosie, there you are! I was beginning to think you weren't coming home."

I bend down and pet Sky as she comes to greet me in her usual, happy way. "Sorry, Mum. I told Russ to tell you I was going to Liam's game. Did you get the message?"

She nods. "I did, yes. I hope you're not relying on that boy too much."

I sigh. Here we go. Okay. I'll bite . . . "What do you mean, Mum?"

81

"Just, well, boys like him won't be around forever. Then, where will you be?"

"What do you mean, 'boys like him?'"

"So good looking. I mean, he could have anyone he wants."

I try to stay in a good mood, I really do, but how can she be so hurtful? I think my newfound confidence from what just happened comes rising to the surface again.

"You know what, Mum? I never normally say anything, but honestly, I've had enough."

"Had enough of what?" she asks, frowning as Russ comes through to the hall.

"Hey, sis."

Just who I need right now. Thank God. "Hey. Stay here for this, Russ, will you?"

He frowns. "Okay."

I turn back to Mum. The fact that I've got Russ at my back is spurring me on. "Mum, I think it's about time I told you how much you hurt me when you say these awful things, and honestly, I've had enough."

"Hurtful things? What hurtful things? I'm never hurtful!"

"Yes, Mum, you are, always commenting about my weight, not letting me eat what I want, commenting on what I'm wearing. You just now basically said that my boyfriend could have anyone he wants, so why would he want me."

She gasps. "I said no such thing."

I nod and sigh at the same time. "Yeah . . . You did."

"I-I honestly don't know what you mean. I do try and help you with your weight. I've been overweight and the 'big girl' all my life, and I know how it feels. I just don't want you to feel the same way as me."

"But you're the one that's making me feel that way. You're the only one that says negative stuff to me. I used to get bullied all day at school then come home and have you making comments like that. Do you have any idea how that made me feel? I didn't want to be at school, and then, I didn't want to be here because of what you might say." A tear runs down my face. I don't want her to see my vulnerability, but my emotions just take over.

Russ walks over and slides an arm around my shoulders. "It's true, Mum. I've heard you so many times. I don't think you realise that what you're saying is hurtful. I definitely know you don't mean to hurt her, but do you ever think about some of the stuff that comes out of your mouth to your teenage daughter? It's bad, Mum. Really bad. I've tried to talk to you about it so many times, but you just wave it off. I knew it would have to come from Rosie. But yeah, Mum. You hurt her a lot."

Mum just looks between Russ and me. She seems genuinely dumbfounded, as though what we're saying is in another language. It's at that moment that I know for sure, 100 percent, that it really is only being said because she thinks it's best for me. She's trying to make me be the best me and trying to get me to not rely on Liam so I won't be heartbroken. She has a screwed-up way of doing it. I mean really. But honestly, I can tell with her face that she doesn't mean to do it. This conversation needed to happen a long time ago.

"I just don't know what to say, love. Why have you never said anything to me before?"

I shake my head. "Because I kept telling myself you were only trying to help. But that doesn't stop it from hurting, and I'm better now, Mum, than I was. I have more confidence. Away from my last school, surrounded by mostly good people at my new one, it's given me the confidence to say something to you."

"I'm so sorry, love. I never thought for one second that I was hurting you. I-I thought I was helping. The thought of you being at school, being so unhappy and then not wanting to come home because of me, well, that breaks my heart."

I swallow, trying my best to hold back the tears.

"It's okay, Mum. Do you think you might be able to think about the things you say first though, maybe be a bit kinder with your words?"

A sob escapes her, and Russ goes over to comfort her. I look at him. Have I done the right thing, saying something about this? Yes, I have. It wasn't my imagination. She's just done it now, for goodness sake. This needed to be said, as upsetting as it is.

She nods while she clings on to Russ. He gives me a sad smile. "Come on. Let's hug it out."

I go over, and all three of us hug while Sky tries to jump up, getting in on the action.

Mum lifts her head. "I'm so sorry, love. I love you so much. I just want you to grow up happy. I will be careful with what I say from now on." She looks at Russ. "Do I do it to you, too?"

He snorts. "No, Mum. I don't have any hang-ups. I wouldn't listen anyway, but our Rosie here is more sensitive. Honestly, I know you're upset—and I hate to see you upset—but she needed to say this a long time ago. I'm glad she's said something."

Mum clings to me so tight and keeps saying sorry. I feel like a huge weight has been lifted off my shoulders, that a cloud—which was weighing me down for so long—has suddenly dissipated. The relief is overwhelming. I spend the evening with Mum. We all have dinner together and then watch TV. For once in my life, I'm feeling truly relaxed and bloody proud of myself. Things will only get better from here. I'm sure of it.

As I'm climbing into bed, I get a message:

So proud of my "girlfriend" today. She's a badass.

I smile. Okay. So, he put girlfriend in quotation marks, but that's because I'm not his girlfriend for real. So, that's okay.

I message him back:

You don't know the half of it, Liam. When I got home, I had it out with Mum, too. Will tell you about it tomorrow. Super proud of myself. I feel like a new person. I have you to thank for this newfound confidence. So, thank you.

I get one back straight away:

That is amazing! I am so proud of you. It needed to be said, though. All okay there now?

Me:**All is fine. Russ backed me up, and Mum apologised.**

Liam:**Well, this deserves a double celebration. So, to celebrate your new status as badass, why don't we have a hot tub night with the bus guys on Friday? Will be fun.**

Hmm . . . Liam in a hot tub. This is a tough decision. Not!

Me:**You have a hot tub?**

Liam:**Yeah. We hardly ever use it. What do you say?**

What do I say? Do I want to hang out with Liam while he's in swim shorts? While I'm in my tankini? Besides the fact that he'll see my oversized hips, thighs and stomach, I'm worried about the fact that I'll see so much of him! It would be fun, though, and I am all about the fun these days, apparently. I think about Riley. She will want to come; she will have to see if she can get a night off at the gym.

I text him back:

Sounds good. You can see what everyone thinks tomorrow.

I get a smiley face back, and then, I put my phone down. Friday night with Liam in the hot tub; Saturday night with him at the party. I'm going to miss him when all this is over. We never actually put a time limit on how long this will go on for, but it can't go on forever. I guess, when he catches up with maths and all the teachers see he's calmed down, that's when we'll end it. Or, if he meets someone else he wants to go out with. Mum is right about that part. I *do* feel like I'm getting too comfortable with him. I don't like that thought at all, so I put it to the back of my mind.

I message Riley:

Liam is going to invite the bus crew to a hot tub party at his place on Friday night. Can you get the night off gym?

Riley:**For Liam? Hell yes! It's presentation night. They have it early cos of all the little ones, so I'll be done by eight. I can come and meet you guys then.**

I feel guilty. I'm having all these feelings for Liam and getting to spend all this time with him when she likes him, too. She has been the best since I moved here, such a good friend. I need not to lose sight of that while I'm in the middle of all this with Liam, or I'm going to lose pretty much the best friend I've ever had. I reply:

Great stuff! Act like you don't know when he asks you tomorrow. Ha-ha!

Riley:**Will do! Yay! I get to see Liam in his swim shorts.**

Yeah, not good.

Chapter Ten

Rosie

Okay. Keep calm.

You've seen him in just is basketball shorts before; this is nothing. You can do this without hyperventilating. I think back to yesterday when I told him and Riley what I'd said to my mum. They were both so proud of me, and when I filled Riley in on my confrontation with Chelsea, she was shocked; she said I've turned into a whole new person. She's right. I do feel like a better version of me for sure. Liam's reaction, though, really got to me. He looked at me with admiration and sadness. I thought about his situation with his mum. He is probably thinking that he can relate. I wish he would talk to his mum about how he's feeling.

It's nearly eight p.m. now and a dark, cold night. I don't see how a hot tub party is going to work at the end of November. I doubt his mum will be there, but will she mind him having a party without her being there? Serves her right if the place gets trashed anyway. She should try being at home more.

My brother is being especially lovely tonight. He isn't going out until later, so he's offered to pick Riley up from her presentation then drop us at Liam's. I thought he'd just shoot me down when I asked about Riley, but he agreed straight away, surprised the heck out of me.

Everyone is going tonight, even Kinsley. I can't believe it. She just said, 'Yeah. Whatever. It'll be cool to hang out in a hot tub'. So, we will see how everyone gets along when they're not on the bus. Of course, they've all known each other longer than they've known me, but it still feels strange. Liam could have just asked his friends over, but I get the feeling that he didn't want to intimidate me by having all his friends there. I'm a little worried about doing the fake relationship acting in front of Riley. I don't want to upset her. I'm in a strange situation. I don't want to tell Liam that Riley has a thing for him because then I'm betraying her trust, but I don't know what to do.

I put on my two-piece tankini under my jeans and jumper and pack a towel and underwear to get changed. I hope I don't freeze to death! I've been in a hot tub before, but it's always been summer. Yes, I know they're hot, but I'll be freezing when I get out. I tie my hair up on top of my head in a messy bun and don't bother with makeup. There's no point when I'll be getting wet.

Russ and I get in the car and head off towards the hall for Riley.

"So, you liking your new school then?"

"I do, Russ. I'm so glad I moved. It's the best thing I ever did."

"You seem a lot happier. It's nice to see. And, you finally said something to Mum; wow. I was so proud of you. I know it wasn't easy, but it needed to come from you, you know? You did it."

"I feel so much happier now that Mum and I had it out. I'm not sure that she'll change. I mean, you could tell from her reaction that she had no idea that she was doing it. Who knows? Miracles happen. I do feel so much happier. I feel so much more relaxed. I never thought I'd get to this point, but the other kids I've met so far at school are great. It was a little hard to believe at first, after... Well, you know. But yeah. They're nice."

"Riley seems cool."

I see him glance sideways at me. "Yeah. She is. She's really nice."

Hmmm... Did he like Riley?

We pull up at the gym where Riley is already outside waiting for us, jumping up and down. I'm not sure if it's to keep warm or with excitement. Maybe both.

She gets in the car. "Okay. Are we mad getting in our swimsuits in this weather? Because I feel like we are."

I laugh, and Russ says, "Yup. You are both out of your minds. Hey, Riley."

"Hey," she says shyly.

I turn to her. "How did the presentation go?"

"Fab! I won a trophy for most points at the comp." She delves around in her bag and pulls out a trophy.

"Wow! That's great. Well done, Riles. You deserve it with how hard you work."

Ross looks behind him to Riley while he's driving. "That's cool; well done."

Okay. He is being way more agreeable to her than he is any other human being.

We pull up in front of Liam's, and we both say bye to Russ.

As we walk up Liam's path, Riley says, "Your brother is so nice."

"Yeah. I've gotta say I think the feeling is mutual."

"What do you mean?"

"Just that he was especially nice to you then. He's not much of a people person."

"Oh, right." She looks thoughtful then shakes it off. "I'm so excited about tonight."

I smile at her. "Me, too."

"Me, three."

"Me, four." Two voices call out from behind us. It's the twins. They're so tall, and I swear they get taller every day. No wonder Edward is on the basketball team. Cooper could be, but I don't think it's his thing. I'm not sure what his thing is.

"Hey. Can you believe we're doing a hot tub in November?" Riley says to them.

Edward laughs. "No, but hey. We're only young once, might as well be crazy."

I knock on the door as Edward's phone beeps. He reads the screen. "Harper's gonna be a little late. She'll be here in 10 minutes."

The door opens, and standing there is my fake boyfriend in the flesh. Well, not literally. He has swim shorts on along with a t-shirt and a jumper. Interesting combo.

"Hey. Come in. Charlie and Kins are already here. They're in the hot tub already."

We follow him through his house. It is enormous, probably double the size of ours, and ours is a decent-sized detached.

We walk through the hall into the kitchen. Then, he takes us into another room, like an orangery with double doors into the garden. In the garden, there is a big gazebo with the hot tub. This is not your run-of-the-mill, inflatable hot tub that fits four. Oh no. This is the top-of-the-range, hard-standing, massive hot tub with built-in lights and room for drinks and built-in seats. It's the kind you would find when you go to a posh hotel for a spa.

"Wow. That is some hot tub, Liam," I say in awe. I can't wait to get in it. Kins and Charlie are talking in there. Well, Charlie is doing most of the talking as usual. Kinsley is either listening or pretending to listen.

"Yeah. It's decent, but I hardly ever use it; no one does. Might as well put it to use."

There are four electric heaters set up on the patio and a wood-burning fire pit.

When we all step outside, there's a mixture of ice-cold air and heat from the stove and heaters. It's surprisingly nice. There are fairy lights set up all around.

Riley speaks. "This is seriously cool."

Liam looks around. "Yeah. I guess my mum had a phase a couple of years back of having friends over. She doesn't bother anymore, but she did this set-up then."

I look at him; maybe I'm the only one that notices the sadness in his voice.

"Your mum home tonight?" I ask quietly.

"Nah. She's out at some work thing. I texted her and told her I was having friends over. It's fine."

He sent her a text. I bet he hardly ever speaks to her. My heart hurts for him.

Cooper and Edward strip off within seconds and get in. Riley is next. I mean, she is used to being in a leotard all the time, so she thinks nothing of showing off her body. Me, on the other hand? Well, this is my worst nightmare. I'm the largest out of all the girls, and they're all in the hot tub already, apart from Harper. So now, I have to strip off with them all being able to see me. Damn. Why did I leave it 'til the last minute to get in? I look at Liam and see that he's taking his jumper off. He must read something on my face.

"Come here."

I walk over to him, aware that everyone is watching us. He leans in and pecks me on the lips. I know it for everyone's benefit, but my body doesn't know that. Tingles shoot through me everywhere.

"You okay?" he asks, his mouth only an inch away from mine.

I nod. "Yeah. Just . . . You know . . . I'm not skinny, and everyone is already in the hot tub. So, they'll see me in my swimsuit. I wish I'd have gotten here before everyone else now, so I could have been in there already when they got here."

He makes a growling sound. "I don't know if it would be a good idea, you and me being alone while you're practically naked in my hot tub."

I gasp. "Liam!"

He laughs. "Sorry." Then, his face goes serious. "Seriously, Rosie, you are beautiful."

I swallow. No one has ever said anything like that to me before.

He leans in even more. "You are. I've never said that to a girl ever. And, you're sexy, and believe me; you have all the curves in all the right places. You

90

have nothing to be self-conscious about. You need to own it. Because you are seriously beautiful."

Wow.

Just wow.

I don't know how to react to that. "No one has ever said anything like that to me before."

"Well, that is a shame and something I would put down to pure, old-fashioned jealousy. Believe me. I know what guys like, and you've got it all."

I can't believe he's saying all this.

"Th-thanks. I don't know what to say."

"You're not used to getting compliments."

I shake my head. "No . . . I'm not. I don't know how to handle them."

"Well, you better get used to them because you're gonna hear them a lot. The sooner you start believing how gorgeous you are, the better."

"You're a right charmer when you want to be, aren't you?" I ask, smiling.

He shrugs. "Just telling the truth, babe." He leans in even closer. "Now, come here and kiss me like you're my girlfriend."

I smile and slide my arms around his neck. This is no hardship whatsoever. I lean forward a little and let him move in the rest of the way. His hands slide around my waist as his lips find mine. The feel of his mouth on mine is exquisite; I can't get enough. He moves his mouth in sync with mine, and electricity shoots all through my body. He slides his hands up my back, pressing my body flat up to his. He deepens the kiss with a groan, and I can feel my heartbeat just about ready to burst out of my chest. I get lost in his kiss.

We hear lots of whistling and yells of "Get a room!" We break off and just maintain eye contact, not saying a word. Is he thinking what I'm thinking? That this doesn't feel like an act anymore? His chest is rising and falling quickly. Is he feeling everything I'm feeling?

I shake my head a little and step away from him. If this doesn't look fake to them, then it doesn't look fake to Riley. I need to back off from him, keep my distance, or she's going to see right through me. The last thing I want to do is hurt her.

I step away from him and start walking towards the hot tub. "Okay. I guess I'll get in."

I glance at Riley, and she's frowning at me, looking deep in thought. Oh, God. Is she onto me?

She swims over to my side of the hot tub where I'm standing. "Come on in, honey. I know why you're stalling, and you're being silly."

I breathe a sigh of relief that she's not frowning because of the kiss. Then, I just feel like a horrible person because she knows I'm self-conscious and is being a good friend. Maybe I should try it sometime.

I take a deep breath and slide off my jeans then pull off my jumper quickly. I get in faster than the speed of light. Oh my... It is heavenly.

I sit down next to Riley and grin. "This is so lovely."

"I know. It's so relaxing." She shouts over to Liam, "Why have we never done this before?"

He glances at me then back to Riley. "I don't know, really. Just never thought about it."

A small part of me wonders if he has done all this just to see me. Then, I wave the idea away. He can have anyone he wants. He isn't the girlfriend type. A thought occurs to me: he's got all the benefits of having a girlfriend without having all the ties and complications. Everyone thinks he has a girlfriend, he gets to kiss me whenever he wants to keep up the facade, yet he doesn't have to be faithful or be places at certain times. He really is living his best life! Is that how he sees all this? I'm supposed to be helping him maintain an image, but am I making a fool of myself? And making a fool of Riley while I'm at it?

I need to back off from him. The evening is a success; everyone gets on, and we have fun. I try to keep my distance from Liam and spend all my time with Riley. We don't need to keep up a front anymore tonight anyway. With that kiss, everyone is convinced, including me there for a second. Eventually, around 10:30, we all decide to call it a night. Riley's dad is picking us up from here at 11 and dropping us home.

We all get dressed and finish off the snacks that Liam had brought out for us. Riley offers to give Kinsley a lift home, too, but she says a friend of hers is picking her up. Charlie is getting a lift with the twins and Harper.

Riley and I are waiting for our lift when Liam comes in, dressed in a t-shirt and shorts, presumably what he sleeps in.

Riley looks up at him. "Thanks so much for tonight; it's been fun."

He nods and smiles at her. I know what her insides are doing right now because it happens to mine every time he smiles at me like that.

"No problem. Glad you've had fun." He looks at me. "Rosie, can I just speak to you in the kitchen for a second?"

I glance at Riley. She looks unsure but says, "It's okay. I'll shout when my dad arrives."

I nod and follow Liam into the kitchen.

He turns around when he reaches a worktop and leans on it. "What's up?"

"Nothing . . . Why?" I have to clear my throat.

"You've been weird with me all night after we kissed. Is something wrong? Did I do something wrong?"

"No, not at all. It's just-just that I feel . . . " How do I put this? I don't want to lay it out there that it seems too real for me. "Nothing is wrong, but while we're on the subject, how long do you think we'll be pretending like this?" I lower my voice so Riley doesn't hear.

His body stiffens. "Why do you ask? Does it matter?"

I shrug. "Maybe now isn't the best time to talk about this. I'll talk to you tomorrow, okay?"

"You're still coming to Connor's party with me though, right?"

I nod. "Yeah. Of course. I'll see you then."

He gives me a short nod, but he's eyeing me suspiciously. He knows something is going on. Just as he's about to say something, we hear Riley shout, "Dad's here!"

I turn to him. "I've got to go."

"Sure. I'll see you out."

He follows behind us, leans in, and gives me a peck on the cheek. I'm relieved that's all he does in front of Riley, especially when it's just the three of us.

Riley and I sit in the back of her dad's car, and Riley turns to me. "It was good tonight, wasn't it?"

I nod and smile at her. "Yeah. I've had fun."

"You and Liam . . . You're still just pretending, right?"

"What do you mean?"

"Well, that kiss? It was hot! I've noticed, too, that when you've been talking to me tonight, he's been looking at you, watching you. A lot."

I shake my head. "No. It's still fake, hun. I know how much you like him."

She nods. "I do, but I'm not under any illusions about him liking me. It's never going to happen with him, but you can't help who you like, right?"

No, you certainly can't. I shake my head and smile at her, squeezing her knee. It's horrible to like someone that doesn't like you in that way. She's a friend that I would be foolish to lose over a boy. I need to remember that.

I get into bed and toss and turn for most of the night, sad when I come to the conclusion that I'm going to have to end this thing. The truth is that I'm just too into it. I like him too much. I thought I could do this, thought I could pretend, but it just feels too real. I feel like everything he does, everything he says, is real, and it's not. I can't carry on like this. I'll go to the party, enjoy pretending for one last time, and then I'll end it. It will be best for everyone. But then why do I feel so sad about it?

Chapter Eleven

Liam

Party time. Thank God. Other than my run this morning, I've been stuck in this house all day. I'm glad to get out. More importantly, I'm glad to be seeing Rosie. I lock up the house and walk around to Rosie's to take her to the party.

What is happening to me? I've never reacted like this with a girl. *Ever.* There have been plenty of girls, ones that I've gone a lot further than I have with Rosie, but she's just different. It's not just about kissing her, touching her—although that part is absolutely incredible. It's about everything else. She's so smart and funny. I love just hanging out with her at her house, taking Sky for a walk, or hanging with her at lunch at school.

I never thought in a million years that I would consider having a girlfriend. What's the point of it all, right? Look at my mum and dad. Like they have any kind of relationship. They never see each other, and they had a kid they barely remember they've had. I just don't see the point. May as well just have fun here and there. Or, that's what I've always thought... Until Rosie. I want to see her all the time, hang out with her, feel her hand in mine, and see her walking across the schoolyard towards me. I can't see her without smiling. Smiling is something I haven't done a lot of for a while.

Maybe I could do it? Me and her . . . Maybe we could be real.

I panicked so much last night when she talked about ending it. Why did she act so weird last night? She was normal right up to the kiss. I mean, I think we both got a little—okay, a lot—carried away with that kiss, but that just proves that there is something there. I don't know; she backed off from me after that.

I'll see how she is tonight and maybe talk to her about it if she's still being weird. I hate the thought of her ending it more than I'd like to admit.

I reach her house. She opens the door before I get a chance to knock. She looks so good. She's wearing jeans and boots with heels. I can't see what top she has on, but she has a purple biker jacket zipped up with a cream scarf and cream gloves. Classy. She has makeup on tonight, and she is good at putting it on. Some of the girls I've been out with before have plastered it on. Why do they do that? Like a guy wants to see that. Rosie has it on to perfection. She's bloody perfect. Her long brown hair is spilling out around her scarf, and she is greeting me with a big smile.

I realise I'm not just happy to see anyone today. I'm happy to see her.

I'm in trouble.

She looks like she's in a good mood, back to normal Rosie which makes me happy. We will have a good night tonight.

"Hey. You look nice." Understatement, but if I said what I actually thought, she would run a mile.

She smiles. "Thanks. So do you."

I don't want to admit that I did make a little bit of extra effort for her tonight. I usually just throw on jeans and any top, but I might have put on my favourite Fendi zip-up top. Might as well look my best. Guys have it lucky, really. There's not much we have to do.

I hold out my hand, she takes it, and we set off walking.

"What did you get up to today?" she asks.

I shrug. I don't want to tell her that I've been on my own all day. I know she gets concerned about that as it is. "Not much. I only got up late then went for a run. What about you?"

"I took Sky out for a walk this morning, and this afternoon, I played badminton with Russ."

"You play badminton?"

She smiles at me. "Yeah. Don't sound so shocked. I do some sports, you know."

"I didn't mean it like that; stop twisting my words. I didn't know you played."

She shrugs. "Yeah. Sometimes. His usual partner dropped out, so I stood in for him. He plays on a team. He's really good. He's just really sporty in general. The opposite of me."

I roll my eyes and ignore that last bit. Always running herself down. "So, did you win?"

She shakes her head. "Er, no. Definitely not, but it was fun."

We arrive at Connor's and just walk in. The usual crowd is there, all the crowd from school, the basketball team, and the hanger-on girls. I like that I'm not turning up on my own, like that I'm with Rosie.

As soon as we step foot inside the door, I hear Harper's voice. "Rosie!" She's stood with Edward as usual. Cooper never comes to these parties; this is the last thing he would want to do.

Harper comes rushing over. "Yay! So glad you're here. Come and hang with us." She looks up at me. "Don't worry. I'll bring her back."

I nod and smile at Harper. Rosie thinks she needed me to fit in. Rubbish. She just needed a little confidence. Everyone likes her. It makes me so mad to think what it must have been like for her at her other school. It's scarred her. She just needed me as a security blanket, a foot in the door. Then, once everyone has gotten to know her, they love her, apart from Chelsea, of course. But that's on me, not her. I hope she's not here tonight; I really can't be bothered with her.

Rosie looks back at me and rolls her eyes as she walks away with Harper, linking her. She pretends not to enjoy it, but I know she does; she likes Harper. I walk over to a few of the basketball team to hang with them for a while.

Half an hour goes by. I think it's time to find Rosie. I came with her after all, and I don't want her to think I'm neglecting her. Although, technically, she's the one that went with Harper, so she should find me. But I'm not about the games. I just want to spend time with her. Yeah. We need to have a chat about this thing becoming real. I really like the thought of it. Stuff my parents. It doesn't have to be like that. I know other relationships that work . . . Well, okay. I can't think of too many at the moment, but I know they're not all as bad as my experiences. I hate that Mum and Dad have got me thinking so cynically at 16.

I walk into the kitchen but can't see her. I step outside to have a look around for her there but can't see her. Where can she be? Maybe the bathroom upstairs? People use that one when the downstairs one is busy. I make my way up there, but the landing looks empty. I'm just about to head downstairs when I hear my name called. I turn around and see Chelsea making her way towards me. *Great. That's all I need.*

I sigh. "Hey, Chelsea."

She sniffs. "Liam, I need to talk to you."

"I think you've said it all, don't you?"

"I'm sorry. I'm sorry I was so mean to Rosie, but it's not her you should be with. It's me." She starts to cry, covering her face with her hands. "You acted as though you liked me, Liam. Do you have any idea how you have made me feel, how you've made me look in front of everyone?"

I feel a little sorry for her. I guess I did make her believe I liked her. Not on purpose because I would never, but I guess she got that impression of me. I never corrected her when I should have.

"You were so mean though, Chelsea. Why do you do it? She's new, too, but that didn't matter to you, did it?"

She shook her head. "All I could feel was jealousy. I was so jealous. I hated it when you gave her your shirt."

Tears are running down her face now, and she swipes them away angrily. "God, I hate that I'm getting upset in front of you."

I sigh. "Look, it's okay, but Rosie deserves an apology."

She starts to really cry, and it bothers me. I hate it when girls cry. "Come here."

She walks over to me, and I wrap my arms around her in a hug, trying to console her. She needs to calm down. I never knew she felt this strongly about me. I would never have hung around with her if I'd known. I'd never liked her like that. She was fine for a make-out session, but that was all it ever was to me.

"Hey . . . Calm down. I'm sorry if I led you on. I never meant to do that."

She looks up from resting her head against my chest, her arms still wrapped around me. "Didn't you like me at all?"

Oh, God. What do I say to that? "Come on, Chelsea. You're gorgeous . . . You know you are."

She smiles. "Thanks."

I see her eyes glance behind me for a second then back up to me. Before I know what's happening, her hand is behind my head and is pushing her mouth on mine. *What the hell?* I don't even realise what is happening. How did it go from consoling her to her trying to kiss me? Crap! I need to stop this.

I grab her arms from around my neck and remove them. "What the hell, Chelsea?"

She grins at me in a way I do not like. "Sorry, Liam. I couldn't help it." She releases me and walks off. Okay. That was surreal. Why did she do that? I thought she was being genuine for a second there, thought she was opening up to me. Thank God Rosie didn't see that. That wouldn't have looked good. Innocent or not, it took me longer than it should have to pull away. Crap. Stay away from Chelsea at all times. That's what I need to do.

I carry on with my hunt for Rosie. I go back into the living room and see Harper. She's having a heated discussion with Edward.

I go over. "Have either of you guys seen Rosie?"

Harper spins around. "Oh, you've missed her, have you, when you had your tongue stuck down Chelsea's throat?"

I go cold. *What the hell?*

"What are you talking about?" I play dumb.

She narrows her eyes at me. "Oh, are you going to tell me that you and Chelsea weren't just kissing upstairs?"

I don't believe this.

"No . . . We weren't."

"So, Rosie was lying? Because she looked pretty upset about it."

"What?"

Edward speaks. "She saw you, dude. She went upstairs looking for you and saw you and Chelsea with your arms around each other, kissing."

And, that's when I knew. That's why Chelsea had done it. She had seen Rosie behind me, and she knew exactly what she was doing. *What a bitch.*

"It's-it's not what it looked like."

Harper huffs, "It never is," and turns her back to me.

Oh, God. I need to sort this out. *Now.*

I look at Edward. "Has she left?"

He nods. "Yeah, dude. She was pretty upset. She took off."

I have a sick-to-my-stomach feeling. This is bad. Very bad. I need to talk to her now.

Chapter Twelve

Rosie

Why, when this was never supposed to be real, do I feel like my heart has been ripped out? I practically run home. But I don't want Mum and Dad to see me back early. I'd have to explain, and I don't want to.

I get home just as Russ is pulling up in the drive.

He sees me and comes over. "Hey, what's wrong? Why are you walking on your own at night?"

I shake my head. "I don't want to talk about it, Russ."

"Has someone . . . Has someone hurt you?"

"What? No. I just . . . Things didn't go well at the party."

"Where is Liam? Why hasn't he seen you home?" He looks around as though expecting Liam to pop out from somewhere.

I snort. "Ha! He's busy."

"Do I need to sort him out, Rosie?"

"What? No! No, it's okay. I just want to go to my room without Mum and Dad seeing me. I don't want them to know I'm upset. Dad will be worried, and Mum will just be, well . . . Mum."

He nods. "I get it. Don't worry. I'll tell them I picked you up and that you're chilling in your room."

I sigh. "Thanks, big bro."

I look at my phone and hand it to him. "Here. Just in case I'm tempted to phone or text someone. Give it back to me in the morning."

He frowns at me but takes it anyway. "Are you sure you're okay?"

"I'll be fine, Russ. Just normal, teenage girl stuff for a change. Nothing like last time. Okay?"

He looks relieved. "Okay, sis. You get up there."

I head to my room and take off my outfit, take my make up off, and look back at plain old Rosie in the reflection. Who did I think I was, running around, going to parties? Hot tub parties for crying out loud! I need just to hide back in the shadows where I belong. I lie back, put my music on, and listen to depressing tunes for a while. I'll make myself snap out of it soon, but right now, I just want to wallow in self-pity.

I must fall asleep like that. When I recheck the time, it's morning. I can hear everyone moving around downstairs. I sigh. I suppose I had better get on with my day. Sky. That's what I need, a good walk with Sky. I look at the time: 9:30. I'll have some breakfast then take her out on a big, long walk.

I get up just as I hear a knock on the door. "Come in."

It's Russ. "Hey. Morning . . . There's someone here to see you."

My heart sinks and soars at the same time. It's got to be him. I wonder if he's tried to phone me.

Before I can say anything, Riley pops her head around the door. "Hey, hun. Can I come in?"

She must see the confusion on my face. "Your brother messaged me from your phone, said you were upset about something? Thought you might need a friend."

Oh, God. Is she the sweetest thing or what? But how do I tell her? How do I tell her that I'm upset that the guy I liked kissed someone else when I thought he was into me? How do I tell her that when she wants him, too? This is just the worst situation. Russ, bless him, thought he was doing the right thing.

I look at him. "Thanks, Russ. That's nice of you."

He shrugs. "No problem."

Riley glances at him and smiles. He looks at her for a little too long. "Thanks for the lift."

"No problem." He smiles and leaves.

She comes in and sits on the bed with me.

"Lift? Russ brought you here?" I ask her.

"Yeah. He's so nice, Rosie. He messaged me to tell me you needed me and then offered to come and pick me up to bring me here."

Oh, he did, did he?

"He's the nicest guy," she adds.

"Yeah. A knight in shining armour that one," I say sarcastically. Nothing to do with the fact that my best friend is gorgeous. He needs to be careful with that. She's not even 16; he is 18, nearly 19. What's he playing at? I can't think about that right now. I've got enough problems to deal with.

"Thanks for coming over."

"Hey. No problem. Why didn't you ring me last night?"

I shake my head. "I-I couldn't."

"What happened at the party?"

I sigh and fill her in on the party, the kiss.

She looks at me blankly. "Had you agreed to stage a break-up or anything?"

I shake my head. "No. Not as far as I'm aware."

She shrugs. "He's out of order for that. He should have told you, but I don't get it. Why are you so upset about the kiss? I mean, he has an on-off thing with Chelsea all the time, and it's not like you guys are really together." She looks confused.

I don't blame her. I'd be confused in her shoes. "Oh, Riley. I can't explain."

She stares at me for a moment. Then, I see realisation dawn in her eyes. "You like him."

Don't cry; don't cry.

I nod. "I tried not to. I tried just to keep it fake, but he's-he's just so nice, you know?"

"Yeah, Rosie. I *do* know. I like him, remember?" Her voice sounds hard. I've never heard it like that before. She's always so happy and kind. An uneasy feeling starts to build inside me.

"I'm sorry. I know you like him. I just couldn't help it."

"I thought you were my friend. I thought you were nice, but you've been kissing him and hanging out with him all this time, telling me it was an arrangement. And, you liked him all along?"

Oh, this is so bad; it sounds so wrong.

"I thought I could keep my feelings under control, not let them take over me."

"You *knew* how much I liked him, how much I hoped he'd notice me one day or whatever. And yeah, I know I'm living in a dream world, but a girl can hope. Then, she tells her friend all about it. She doesn't expect the friend to go after the guy she likes."

"I didn't mean to hurt you, Riley. It doesn't matter now anyway, does it? He's made how he feels perfectly clear. It has just been fake to him all along. I am an idiot."

"Yeah, you are," She barks. "In more ways than one."

"Please don't be mad at me."

"Sorry, Rosie, but it isn't all about you. No wonder girls were so mean to you at your other school if you treated them like this."

I gasp. "You-you can't mean that."

"It makes me wonder what exactly you did to them for them to be so mean to you. You obviously don't know what it means to be a friend, do you?" She stands up to leave.

"Please don't leave. Let's sort it out," I plead.

"There's nothing to sort out. What's been done can't be undone. I hope he's worth throwing a friend away for." She storms out.

I hear the front door close and then hear Russ's car. He must be taking her back home.

I burst into tears. This is all wrong; everything is going wrong. I just wanted to fit in at my new school, and I was doing fine. But then, Liam happened. I had a lovely friend in Riley, and I've just blown it. I've messed everything up.

After a while, I get up and go downstairs. Just as I'm heading towards the kitchen to face everyone, Russ opens the front door.

"How was she?" I ask.

"She was upset . . . What happened?"

I sigh. "I've just messed up big time, that's what. She's, like, the nicest person. She welcomed me into her group of friends and has been so nice, and now I've hurt her."

"Please tell me this isn't about Liam..."

"Do you want me to lie?"

"Oh, Rosie. What has he done?"

"Doesn't matter. It's what I've done that's important. I fell for him when I knew I shouldn't. I couldn't help it, and now Riley hates me. I've been so selfish. I should have just turned Liam down right from the beginning."

He sighs and runs his hands through his hair. "Give her a few days. She's pretty upset, but I'm sure, in a few days, she will have calmed down enough to hear you out."

I won't hold my breath, but he's only trying to help. "Thanks, Russ, and thanks for bringing her over. I know you were only trying to help."

"Yeah . . . Messed up on that one, didn't I?" He walks over and hugs me. "I know how strong you are, Rosie; sort it out. Do what needs to be done. You can handle anything after last year."

I hug him back and try not to cry again, grateful that someone has faith in me.

I get breakfast, make conversation with Mum, and get out of the kitchen as fast as I can. I grab my phone and head upstairs to get ready to take Sky out. I check my phone. I have so many messages.

Harper: **Are you okay, hun?**

Harper: **Liam just came downstairs looking for you. I told him what you'd seen. Arse.**

There are messages between Russ and Riley which just make me feel bad.

Then Liam: **It's not what you think.**

I need to speak to you.

Can I see you?

Answer me, please. Let me explain.

There are three missed calls from him. I'm glad I didn't have my phone. I might have caved and spoken to him.

I message him back:

Leave me alone. I take it from last night that our fake thing is over. See you at the bus stop Monday.

My phone rings straight away; it's him. I reject the call and then turn my phone off. I need to clear my head. I take Sky for the longest walk, trying to think things through, trying to think what my next move will be. I come to the conclusion that I need to not give up on Riley. I'm not going to lose a good friend over this; she needs to see that I'm not selfish. Alright, it might look like I've been super selfish, but I can prove her wrong. I also need to speak to Liam, clear the air before school because the last thing I need is him talking to me on the bus on Monday when everyone can hear.

I need to cut all ties with Liam. He won't be bothered anyway. He has Chelsea to keep him busy.

I decide to call around at his house, see if he's in, and just hope to goodness his mum isn't there.

Chapter Thirteen

Liam

Right. That's it. She won't talk to me, so I'm going to go around to her house and hope that she agrees to see me. I need to sort this out now. I don't want to wait until Monday, and I don't want this to be over. Anything but. This has just made me realise how much I like her. I think it happened gradually; I don't know when the heck it happened actually, but I do know that the thought of not spending time with her makes me feel gutted. I love her company, not just the physical. We have fun, and she makes me feel wanted, important. She listens when I talk; I don't have much of that.

I get dressed and head downstairs. It's one of those rare moments when Mum is home. I'm in no mood for Mum. I go into the kitchen to get a banana and pour a glass of juice.

"Hello, stranger," Mum says as she walks into the kitchen. She's dressed in her gym things; she's probably heading out again soon.

"Hi," I say in a low voice.

"I feel like I haven't seen you in ages."

"That's because you haven't."

"I know, I've been pretty busy lately. Your dad is due home soon, so you'll have two parents again for a little while."

I've had enough of Mums' bull. "I don't even have one parent around, Mum. What makes you think I'll notice when the other one comes back for a week?"

"Blimey, someone got out of bed on the wrong side."

Do I tell her how I feel? If Rosie has taught me anything these last few weeks, it's that I'm not insignificant, that people can care about me. She cared about me. What kind of parent just leaves their 16-year-old son to their own devices? If I don't tell her, how will she ever know how I feel? Obviously, the parenting gene skipped my mum. She should know that her son is hurting, but she doesn't.

"You don't know me enough to comment on my mood, do you?"

She looks shocked. "What do you mean by that?"

"You remember that you have a son, right? Because to me, it looks as though you have forgotten about me altogether. You seem to prefer pretending that I don't exist."

She gasps. "That's a terrible thing to say."

"Yeah? And, how did you get on at my parents evening? Did they say I was doing okay?" The thing is, if she *had* bothered to turn up to parents evening, she would have heard about how much better I'm doing, but she didn't bother.

A look of guilt flashes over her. "Well, I'm sorry about that. I couldn't make it; I got caught up at work."

"Yeah. You do that a lot. You know what, Mum, forget I said anything. You just carry on as you always do, and I'll just look after myself. I guess you've taught me the lesson early that you are on your own in this world and to survive, you have to look out for number one. Got that message loud and clear. I have to go."

I don't give her time to respond to that. She's in shock. I never usually say anything to her; I just let her go on in her own, little, selfish life without having to give me a thought. I brush past her and leave the house. I need some air. This is turning out to be a terrible weekend. Rosie is being distant with me after that fantastic kiss, then there's last night, and now this.

I walk around the corner. Knowing I need to go and see Rosie, I head in that direction, but I need to calm down first. I need to get Mum out of my head and think rationally about what I'm going to say to Rosie without getting wound up about it.

I need to get across *calmly* how I feel about her.

When I turn the corner towards her house, I spot her with Sky. She's heading towards my house from the other direction.

"Rosie!" I shout to get her attention. I start running to catch her up. She turns around and spots me. Jeez, I hope she did not train her dog to kill on command. If she has, I'm a goner because the look she gives me is anything but friendly. "Rosie, wait up!" I catch her, and Sky starts wagging her tail when she sees me.

Rosie stops when Sky starts pulling to get at me and sighs. Turning around, she says, "I was just coming to find you, actually. We need to talk." Her voice sounds cold, almost robotic.

Where exactly do I start?

I kneel to pet Sky. "Come here, girl. Who's a good girl? You're so good." Sky is so happy to see me. *Thanks Sky. I knew you'd be on my side.*

"Yeah? Good. I was coming to see you."

"I just wanted to confirm that this fake thing, whatever it was, is done now," she says, looking down at me.

I stand up, towering over her. "You need to let me explain."

"There is nothing to explain because whatever you say wouldn't change the fact that I need to end it with you."

"Not even if I have a perfectly reasonable explanation?" I'm sure I can get her to believe that the kiss wasn't what it looked like.

She shakes her head. "No. Not even then. It doesn't matter anyway, does it? This thing . . . It wasn't real. It was just fake, so now it's done. We don't need to stage a break-up at school because everyone knows about you kissing Chelsea last night when you were supposed to be at the party with me. So, I think that's me adequately humiliated, don't you?"

"I didn't . . . I wasn't. Just let me speak."

"It doesn't matter, Liam. That's what I'm trying to say. This ends now."

"What if I like you?" I need to tell her how I feel.

The cold look in her eyes falters. *Doubt.* I need to carry on. "I like you, Rosie. I don't want it to be fake. I want it to be real."

She shakes her head, more to herself than to me. "I-I don't."

"You sure about that?"

She looks down at her feet then back up to me, her eyes so full of anguish I feel it in my gut. "I am sure. Yeah. I don't like you like that. I get on with you, Liam, as a friend, but it was always just fake for me. I'm sorry."

I look down at her. "I don't believe you. I don't believe that we were all fake. I think all of it was real. *You* were real."

"Just please leave me alone, Liam," she says with desperation.

"No. Look me in the eyes and tell me you don't like me, that you don't want us to be together."

There is pain written all over her face, and it's killing me. She doesn't say anything.

"The kiss . . . It wasn't . . . She kissed me."

Her face closes down again. Balls! That wasn't the right thing to say.

"I don't want to be with you; let's just leave it at that. I hope we can be civil on the bus. Otherwise, it will be awkward for everyone else. We have Christmas break soon anyway. So then, new year, a fresh start, and all that. I'd like to say thank you for helping me fit in, but I don't think it's gone so well for me. At least I managed to help you with your work, so some good did come out of it."

She turns around and walks away.

Okay. I'm getting angry now. How can she just dismiss everything like this? "So, that's it? You won't even let me explain? You think I would do that to you? I wouldn't. Jeez, you mustn't think much about us, about what we have or had, that you can just dismiss it so quickly."

She turns around, looking so sad. If she's sad, I can make it better. Why won't she let me in?

"I'm sorry, Liam, but whether or not last night happened, I still need this to end."

"Why?" I just don't get it.

"It was never meant to be anything more than a crutch for me."

"So, I was your crutch, and that's it?" Does she know how much she's hurting me right now? Have I misjudged her? Was she acting all along when I thought it was as real as it gets?

"I'm sorry, Liam." She turns and walks away. I let her this time. I mean so little to her. I guess I had better let her go.

Chapter Fourteen

Rosie

I walk up to the bus stop with a feeling of dread inside me. Why did he have to be early? He's stood there with one hand in his pocket, head down, looking at his phone in his other hand. He hears me approach and looks up. He looks right through me. I feel it like I would feel a knife to the chest. I guess I deserve that look. I mean, yeah, he kissed Chelsea, which is bad, but I won't even let him explain. He doesn't understand that it's because of Riley, and I can't tell him. So, let him think that I gave up on him. They kissed anyway, whether I want to believe it or not. I saw it with my own eyes.

He looks back to his phone without saying anything. So, this isn't awkward at all. Then, Riley comes around the corner. She looks at Liam, then me, and then just stands at the side of us both. "Hey, Liam."

He looks up, frowning, and then looks at me. He probably thinks she doesn't know about Saturday night, seeing as she's my friend and wouldn't be talking to him if she did know.

"Hey, Riley. How's it going?"

She smiles at him. "Great. How was your weekend?"

Riley, come on. Being outright mean to me just isn't her.

He looks at me uncertainly. "I've had better to be honest."

"I heard you had a great time."

"Whatever, Riley," he says and just carries on looking at his phone.

Okay. I need to pluck up the courage to speak to her. I said I wasn't giving up on our friendship, and I meant it. "Riley, can I talk to you?"

She shakes her head. "I don't think we have anything to say, do you?"

"Actually, yeah. I have a lot I want to say to you."

Liam looks up. "What's happened with you two?"

"Nothing. Well, nothing you need to worry about anyway." Riley smiles sweetly at Liam.

Liam looks at me with concern but doesn't say anything. Thankfully, just as the others are walking up, the bus pulls up. Riley doesn't sit in her usual seat. She goes and sits next to Harper.

Harper smiles over at me uncertainly. Okay. So, everyone is wondering what is going on on the bus today.

It doesn't get any better at school either. I just keep my head down and try to get on with my lessons as best I can. How can I show Riley that I'm sorry? I try to rack my brain, to think of something. Alone at lunchtime, I go to the library and decide to write her a letter. Seeing as she won't hear me out, if I put it all down on paper, I have more chance of her reading it. I think about what I want to say. Then, I start to write:

Riley,

Please read this. You won't talk to me, and I want to explain things. I'm so sorry you feel that I betrayed you. I would never go out of my way to hurt you.

I think I need to explain things a little further about how things were for me before Arrowsmith so that you might understand how much I appreciate you.

The girl I spoke with you about, the one that was mean to me... I told you she was popular, and everyone listened to her. Her boyfriend had apparently said something nice about me once, and she was jealous. Once. That's all it took for her to make my life a living hell. The first thing she did was get one of the boys to come up to me and pretend to ask me out. I fell for it, said yes, got ready for a date, and actually turned up at where we were supposed to meet only to have her turn up and laugh at me with her friends. Stood there humiliated, I had to walk away, totally alone. Do you know what it's like not to have anyone to talk to? It's soul-destroying. That was just the beginning of a long line of nasty tricks. She would take stuff out of my backpack in class, so that when I turned up to a lesson, I would get punished for not having the right equipment. She would wait for me after detention to talk to me, tell me how ugly I was, how fat, how no guy would ever be interested. She never laid a finger on me; she wasn't that stupid. She was smart about it all actually. That's how it went on for so long. Everyone was scared

to talk to me. I used to go and eat my dinner in a far corner of the hall on my own, stood up. No one wanted to sit with me. It was the darkest time I hope I will ever know. I've never been close to Mum, as you know, so the only person I could talk to was Russ. Thank God for my brother. No one should have to go through that. But I'd like to think it made me stronger.

But you know what it made me realize? To be grateful. Grateful for every good thing that comes into my life. And, I know we haven't known each other that long, Riley, but I'm grateful for you. You have been nothing but kind and friendly to me, helping me fit in when you didn't have to do anything. I owe you. I owe you big time. Do you have any idea how hard it was for me to start a new school? Of course, you do, because you were there to help me through it, even though you hardly knew me. You are the sweetest person I have ever met. I don't want to lose your friendship. I will prove to you that I can be a good friend.

I can start by showing you that, no matter what, I won't talk to Liam again. I'll say hello, but no matter what my feelings are for him, I won't let them go any further. It's over. I've told him it's over. I'm so sorry I fell for him. I tried not to. Believe me. I tried.

Please let me make it up to you. I don't care how long it takes, but I know a good friend when I see one. I don't intend to let it go.

Rosie xx

I fold it up, planning to put it in her backpack on the bus. Then, she should find it when she's doing her homework.

I'm heading back to lunch when I bump into Harper. "Oh . . . Hey, Harper."

"God, who killed your kitten?"

I smile at her. "Sorry. I'm having a monumentally bad day."

"Yeah? Well, I'm going to make it better. Have you spoken to Liam about Chelsea?"

I shake my head. "Liam and I are done. Whatever happened, we're over."

"Yeah, but have you heard what he's telling everyone?" she asks.

"What? No. What's he saying?" I know I shouldn't be interested, but I can't help it.

"Just that Chelsea pounced on him on purpose when she saw you behind him, and that he pushed her off. That she is a manipulative little witch, and he is making it clear to everyone that they are not, or never will be, an item. And, that he's not interested."

"Wow. He said all that?" Why does it make me feel so happy but so devastated at the same time? Because it doesn't matter. I can't be with him anyway.

"Yeah. It's so cool; he's really making it clear to everyone. So, you can forgive him now, right? It was all a misunderstanding?"

I smile sadly. "I can't, Harper, no. We're over . . . There are other things going on, too, so it's for the best anyway."

"But I've seen how you look at him. It's like how I look at the Salvatore brothers. I mean, Damon... Stefan... Which one to choose? You look at him like that. You're really into him. Anyone can see it, and it sounds like he's as into you as you are him."

"Why? Has he said anything about me?"

She shakes her head. "Well . . . No, but the fact that he made it clear about Chelsea tells us something, doesn't it?"

"It doesn't tell me anything other than he's not into Chelsea. Sorry, hun. I know you were probably hoping that you were giving me good news, but Liam and I are finished."

She shakes her head. "This isn't finished yet. I'm not convinced. Watch this space." She flouts off before I can say anything else. God, I hope doesn't interfere.

I go home. There is barely any speaking on the bus. I put my headphones on and watch Netflix numbly. Liam isn't on the bus, and neither is Edward. So, I presume they have basketball practice. I get home and go through the motions, hoping that I might get a call from Riley when she finds the letter, but nothing. I go to school the next day. It's pretty much the same again. Liam is not talking to me. Riley is not talking to me. It's agonising. It's two weeks away from Christmas, and I have a feeling I'm going to have the worst one ever. But it's all my own doing.

Chapter Fifteen

Liam

This week just sucks ass. It's the worst week ever. Rosie won't even look at me. I don't get it. I've made it clear to anyone that will listen that Chelsea staged the kiss, that I'm not interested. I was hoping, when she heard, that she would come back to me. Or, at least start talking to me again. Obviously, I wasn't as important to her as I'd hoped.

I'm an idiot. Why would someone like her want to go out with someone like me anyway? She's way out of my league.

At least I've got the game tonight. It's a final, a big deal. That'll take my mind off things and should draw in a good crowd. I shake my head. I need to get to tech, finish off my project. I'm not even sure that I want to finish it off, but I have to do it.

I hear someone running behind me, calling my name. I turn around. Riley is trying to catch up to me.

"Hey, Riley. What's up?"

She has a piece of paper in her hand. "I need to talk to you about this."

"Sure. Come into tech with me. We can talk there." We go into the classroom, and she shuts the door. It's weird. Riley's never wanted to talk to me before. Dare I hope that it's something about Rosie?

"Everything okay?"

She shakes her head. "No. No, it's not."

"Is it Rosie? She's okay, right?"

"Kind of. I need to tell you something, but first, I need to tell you something embarrassing about myself. I'm kind of wanting your agreement that, once I tell you this, you will put it out of your mind forever."

"Okay. You're worrying me now, but yes. I will forget what you tell me unless it's that you've murdered someone or something."

"Nothing quite so bad. What it is is that, for a few years now, I've . . . God, this is hard . . . I've had a little crush on you."

I raise my eyebrows. "Have you?"

"Well, yeah. Did you realise?"

"I had absolutely no idea. You've barely ever talked to me." I don't know why this has anything to do with Rosie, but I had no idea she had a thing for me.

"Yeah. I've been a little shy around you." She blushes.

"Is this you asking me out?" If she is, she has guts; trouble is, I'm only interested in one girl right now.

"What? No!" She looks horrified. "No. I wanted to talk to you about Rosie. She likes you, Liam."

I give a little laugh. "Think you might be mistaken there. I know you know about the fake thing. You were the only one that knew. Well, turns out she's an outstanding actress because I thought she might actually like me there for a minute. But it was all just an act."

"No, it wasn't. She likes you."

"You need to speak to her. I can tell that something is going on with you guys. We've all noticed on the bus that you're not speaking to her, but if you ask her, I think you'll find out that she's not interested."

"Or, what it could be is that I found out that she liked you for real—not just pretend—and I was so annoyed with her that I fell out with her about it."

I'm so confused right now. "Riley, that doesn't make any sense. Why would you fall out with her just because she liked me?"

Riley flushes. "That would be the part where I'm selfish. You see, I've been calling *her* selfish and self-centred since all this happened when the truth is that it is *me*. I was mean to her because I've seen the way you look at her. It's not fake for you anymore, is it?"

I shake my head. God, am I being that obvious? "No. I like her for real."

She nods her head sadly. "Thought so. I guess I didn't like it. You noticed her, but you didn't notice me. This is mortifying, by the way, talking to you about this."

"Thanks for telling me this, Riley, but it doesn't change anything. She doesn't want to be with me."

"See, I think that's where you are wrong. She wrote me this letter, you see. I think she *does* like you but wants me to be her friend. I think she's backing off from you, so I'll be friends with her."

I frown. "I'm getting lost in all this girl crap. Tell me what's going on in her head and what I need to do."

"Okay. She likes you but thinks I won't be her friend if she lets you know it. I will find her, tell her that I'm okay with it and that she can be with you."

"I think she's still mad about Chelsea kissing me."

Riley shrugs. "I can't answer that. We haven't exactly been on speaking terms lately. But she's probably heard, like all of year 11 have, that Chelsea threw herself at you. You've made it pretty clear, your feelings on Chelsea."

I nod. "So, I guess I need to speak to Rosie then."

"Yeah, but I need to speak to her first, tell her she's still got a friend. If she'll have me, that is."

"I know this can't have been easy for you, telling me all this. I'm sorry, Riley. I had no idea that you saw me that way." I lean into her. "You see, unless you actually tell a guy outright, we're pretty rubbish at reading the signals."

She laughs. "Yeah. Well, doesn't matter now, does it? I'll get over it. I'll bear that in mind for the future though. So, you'll talk to Rosie?"

"I will. Not sure what the outcome will be, but I'll try again."

She grins. "Thanks, Liam. I'm going to go. I need to try and find her. I don't know when she put this letter in my bag. I've only just seen it."

I watch her leave, my head nearly exploding with the amount of information that has just come my way. If I can convince her about the kiss, might I be able to be with her for real? Actually be with her, hold hands with her while we're walking her dog, kiss her, hang out in the hot tub with her, watch games with her dad and brother? I need this to work. Hope starts to build inside me. I go to my workbox that Teach has put to one side for me and get out what I've been working on. I get an idea. It's a little crazy, but I'm feeling a little crazy. If it fails, well . . . I'll give everyone entertainment and gossip fodder for a week or so. I'm gonna do it. I need to get to work. I have a lot to do.

I need Harper's help, though. I message her:

I don't know how your gonna do it, but I need Rosie to be at the game tonight. Please. I will owe you BIG TIME if you pull it off. Make anything up. I don't care, just get her there.

Then, I get to work.

Chapter Sixteen

Rosie

I go into the library. Spending another lunchtime alone then. I sit down and get out my book. Just as I take a bite into my very boring, wholemeal salad sandwich prepared by my loving mother, Riley comes bursting through the door. She's holding something in her hand. I think it's my letter.

"Oh, good. I've found you," she pants.

"Yeah. Here I am. Living the dream." I smile at her. I point to her hand. "Is that my letter?"

"Yeah. I've only just found it. When did you put it in my bag?"

Hope ignites inside. If she only just found it, that means that she hasn't been ignoring it for two days. Please let her be ready to forgive me.

"I sneaked it into your bag on Monday night on the way home from school. I thought you'd have found it that evening, and you were just ignoring it."

"No, I literally just found it now. I'm so sorry. I've been such a bitch." She comes and sits down at the side of me.

I'm shocked. "What? You're not the bitch. I'm the bitch. I'm the one that fell for the guy you liked."

"Exactly. God, if anyone knows that you can't choose who you fall for, it's me. I wouldn't have chosen to crush on the same guy for three years, would I? One that doesn't even know I'm alive?"

"God, Riley, I'm so sorry." I feel so bad.

"Just let me finish, Rosie. It was just jealousy, pure and simple. I saw the way he was looking at you. I wanted to believe it was part of the act, but no one is that good of an actor. He is *so* into you, and I hated you for it." She cringes as she says that then holds up her index finger and her thumb. "Just a little bit. I'm sorry I took it out on you. You haven't been selfish. I mean, I wish you'd have talked to me about it, about your feelings, but I understand why you felt you couldn't. You were protecting me."

I nod.

She carries on. "Anyway, I guess I just wanted to say that I hope we can go back to being good friends because we get on so well, and I don't want a boy to come between us. Now that I've calmed down and stopped being an idiot anyway."

I feel so much relief. "It means so much that you've said that, and I promise. It's done now with Liam. Nothing more will happen. I won't go near him."

She sighs. "Aw, well, that is a shame. You see, I've just been to see Liam and told him why you backed off from him in the first place and said that he needed to do something about you two being apart."

I freeze. "You did *what*?"

"I told Liam that you backed off because of me. I even told him about my crush which was pretty embarrassing. Then, I told him that I was coming to find you to tell you it was okay, that I wouldn't be childish and fall out with you if you went out with each other for real."

"Oh, my God. So, Liam thinks I like him for real?" I feel like I'm going to throw my sandwich back up.

"Well, yeah. But you do, right?" She looks confused.

"I do, but I-I don't know. I'm terrified that he knows."

"All I told him is that I was the reason you backed off. He thinks you're mad about the Chelsea kiss. I told him that I didn't know how you felt about that, which I don't. We haven't spoken. So, he said he's going to speak to you later." She relaxes back and takes a deep breath. "Phew! It feels good to get all that off my chest."

I am still gobsmacked. I just stare at her.

She looks up at me. "So, we're good?"

I nod. "We're good . . . Of course, we're good. I missed you."

"I missed you, too. Come on. Let's hug it out." She leans over and hugs me, and I hug her back, nearly crying with relief, so happy that she's my friend again and that she's okay.

She breaks off from me. "Jeez, I might be able to relax now. I've been running around everywhere. Come on. Let's go have our dinner in the yard before the bell goes."

I nod, nervous that I might see Liam again and what might happen. She must see my hesitation. "Don't worry. He's in the tech lab."

We make our way into the yard, and Harper comes running over to me. "Rosie! There you are! I've been looking for you everywhere. Is there any chance you can come with me to the basketball game tonight? Anna and Heidi have had things come up, and I promised Edward that I'd go. It's the final. It's a massive deal for him; he'll fall out with me if I don't go, so I'll be sat there on my own for two hours. *Please*? Please come. You, too, Riley?"

I nod. "Yeah. No problem. Just let me text Dad, let him know I'll be late." I feel a little uneasy about going to the game, but Liam won't know I'm there. He won't expect me, so he won't be looking for me. Plus, his mind will be on the game.

She looks so relieved. "Thanks! You're a star. What about you, Riley. You don't have practice tonight, do you?"

"No. I'll come; why not? It's the final, and there will be lots of hot basketball players for me to ogle. So, sure. Gotta find me a new man to stalk now." She laughs.

I'm so happy that she is at a place that she can make a joke about it.

I don't see any of them for the rest of the day. I have English and Geography, but they're not in those lessons with me. I'm filled with nervous anticipation all afternoon, wondering if Liam will talk to me if he sees me. I know this final is important to the school. There will be a lot of people watching I think, so he will probably be focused on that. Then, hopefully, he'll be celebrating with the team afterwards. I try not to think about it. What if he's decided all this is not worth the effort anyway? Maybe he'll just move on. There are plenty of girls at Arrowsmith High that would love to be next in line.

I go to meet Harper and Riley. We sit down on the bench that we sat on last time we watched the game which just brings back bittersweet memories. I wish I didn't have quite as good a view of Liam.

Harper is wriggling around in her seat. I turn to her. "Harper, oh, my God, calm down."

She giggles. "I can't; I'm just so excited."

I look at Riley as if to say, "Come on. It's a high school basketball game, not the FA cup final." I pat Harper's knee. "I need to get you out more," I say jokingly.

She laughs a nervous laugh. Okay. Weird.

The next minute, I see Harper's friends, Heidi and Anna, coming towards us. I frown. I thought they'd had something come up. I turn to Harper. "Heidi and Anna are here. I thought they couldn't make it?"

She looks over at them heading our way. "Oh . . . They must have changed their plans . . . Yay." She jumps up, running over to them before they can reach us and starts talking to them quietly.

I turn to Riley. "Okay. Harper is weirder than usual today."

Riley just shrugs. "Same amount of weirdness to me."

The players start spilling onto the court. My eyes immediately fleet around everyone, looking for my guy. *My guy.* The one I want to be my guy, anyway. I can't see him anywhere. I hope he's not injured. I just presumed he'd be playing, but maybe not. I desperately look around, hoping for him to appear, but he doesn't. They all warm up, and my heart sinks. Where is he? Is everything okay? I can't believe how disappointed I feel. I was pining to see him, obviously. I just didn't realise how much.

The PE teacher, who coaches the basketball team, comes to stand in the middle of the court. He motions for everyone to be quiet. Both the teams line up on each side of the pitch, facing each other.

He starts to speak. "Okay. So, something a little different is happening before the game today. I've had a special request."

I look at the team. They're all grinning and looking around the crowd. Are they looking for someone?

He carries on. "I don't normally encourage this kind of thing, but he's pulling in a favour. Lord knows I owe him a few, seeing as he's my lead scorer."

My heart lurches. Isn't Liam his lead scorer?

"Liam, son, you wanna come and do your thing? These people don't have all day. There's a game to play."

My heart starts beating so fast, I feel like it's going to come out of my chest. What is he playing at?

Liam runs onto the pitch, and the rest of the team starts cheering and whooping. Harper starts bouncing up and down on the bench.

Liam turns to talk to the crowd. "Hey, everyone. Sorry. I'll be real quick." He has something in his hand, but I can't see what it is. "Harper, I hope you haven't let me down."

He scans the crowd, for some reason looking for Harper.

She waves and shouts, "As if."

He grins at her and then his eyes find mine. There is an intensity in them that I've never seen before. His look takes my breath away.

"Rosie... The reason I'm doing this in front of everyone here today is so that everyone knows the score. There is no other girl I am interested in other than you. I want you. I won't go into details, but I will tell you this: it's only you. I never thought I would want a girlfriend, never thought that I would do something so sappy as this, but here I am. Truth is, Rosie, I'm in love with you."

I hear lots of people gasp all around the gym, but I barely register it. Did he? Did he just say he's in love with me?

He starts walking over to me. I'm only two benches up, so he doesn't have to go far to get to me. He stands in front of me. "Come here."

I swallow, nervous. Everyone is looking at me. Talk about wanting to blend in, fit in. I am totally standing out right now, completely out of my comfort zone. But the look on his face... God, I can't do anything but what he's asking me to do. I step out onto the gym floor.

He grabs my hand and says, lower, "I love you, Rosie. I want you to be my girlfriend for real. Everything that we did when it was fake, it was all real for me. Be my girlfriend?" He looks so hopeful and scared. God knows what look must be on my face. I think about Riley, and I turn around to see if she's watching, which, of course, she is. She gives me a nod and a shaky smile and blows me a kiss. I know how hard this must be for her.

I turn back to him. She's just given me the go-ahead. I can be with him if I want to be.

"Here." He hands the thing to me that was in his hand, wrapped in tissue.

I open it up and gasp. It is a perfectly sculpted rose made of wood, the one he said he was making. The detail in it is astounding; the amount of work and care he must have put into it, I can't even imagine. He is so talented.

I look up at him. "For me?"

"A beautiful rose for my beautiful Rosie." He smiles at me.

I look down at it again.

"Be my girlfriend?"

I grin at him. "I'd love to!"

I hear someone behind me mutter, "She's smiling; it must be good."

He grins and pulls me into a hug, kissing my cheek. "You won't regret this, *girlfriend*."

I lean back. "I like the sound of that."

He closes the distance between us, and his mouth finds mine. The crowd starts cheering. It's the most surreal experience of my life. It's a quick kiss, probably longer than it should be in front of a crowd, but lovely all the same and full of meaning.

I break off from him and lightly push him away. "Come on. You've got a game to play."

The coach shouts. "Okay. Okay. What is this, a teen movie? Come on! Let's play!"

The crowd goes crazy. It was already a good atmosphere, but after what just happened, after what Liam just did for me in front of everyone, the atmosphere is even more electric.

I sit down as the girls crowd around me. They gush over the rose, amazed by his talent. There's only really his tech teacher that knows about his talent. And me. I look over and see Liam run over to his tech teacher who's here to see him play. He gives him a high five. He is the best teacher, the only one that has had faith in Liam all the way through.

*****

The final whistle goes. It was a close one, but we win! Liam has the best game and comes running over to me with his shirt. Shirtless. My hot, basketball player, non-fake boyfriend is stood in front of me, shirtless. Wow. I give him a grin and quick kiss on the mouth. I could get used to this.

"Congratulations, Liam."

He waves his hand dismissively. "Ah, I'd already won before the game even started."

I smile at him. God, I love him, too. I really do. I love him.

"Go on. Go celebrate with your teammates."

"We're heading to Bella's to celebrate. You'll come?"

I shake my head. "You celebrate with the guys. I'll see you later if you like?"

He looks disappointed. "Some of the other girlfriends are going. I want to show you off . . . Please?"

Harper speaks up. "I'm going. You can come with me?"

I look back at him. "Okay then. I'll come, do my girlfriend duties and all that." I roll my eyes as though it's a chore when it couldn't be further from the truth. I grin at him.

"Great. Come outside with me first, though."

"Why?"

He grins and winks at me. "You know why . . . "

Butterflies dance around in my stomach. I *think* I know why.

He grabs my hand and walks me outside the sports hall. People are milling around, leaving, and kids are getting into their parents' cars. He pulls me around the side of the sports hall, the side that has trees lining it. It's private.

He pulls me around and then nudges me backwards so my back is against the wall. "Finally, I've got you all to myself."

His face is so close. I can feel his breath on me. He must be freezing; it's so cold, and he is hot from his game.

I look down at his mouth, willing him to kiss me. He leans in even closer, teasing me. "So, how do you feel about me being your real boyfriend?"

I reach up and put my hand against his cheek. He closes his eyes and takes a deep breath in.

"I feel really good about it," I whisper, my voice full of emotion.

He opens his eyes. "Do I need to explain? About Chelsea?"

I shake my head. "No. You've made the facts of that pretty clear."

He gives a little nod and leans in, muttering near my lips, "So, you won't mind if I kiss you now, then? For real?"

I wind my other hand around his neck. "Just so you know, Liam, it was always real for me."

He leans back a little to look into my eyes, looking from one to the other. "Me, too," he says softly.

His mouth is finally on mine, and we kiss. He winds his hands around my waist, pressing his body flat against mine against the wall; there is no space between us. He tilts his head to give himself better access and deepens the kiss, our mouths melding as though they were made for each other. I revel in the feel of him surrounding me. The scent of him is intoxicating, the taste, the feel of his mouth moving against mine, and his hands working their way up my back. I feel like I'm in heaven.

He breaks off the kiss and starts to butterfly kiss down my neck, concentrating on the part where my neck meets my shoulder, giving me open-mouthed kisses there, and I feel his tongue dart out, sending shivers all over my body. Then, his mouth finds mine again.

We break off after a time, and I look at him. This gorgeous guy is really mine. I still can't get my head around it.

"You know," I speak, my voice breaking, "I love you, too."

He rests his forehead against mine. "God, you have no idea how good it is to hear you say that. I was terrified I was going to make a fool out of myself before. I was terrified you were going to turn me down."

I grin. "You know, I've never been a non-fake girlfriend before."

"Well, that's just fine, because I've never been a non-fake boyfriend before. I'm sure we'll work it out together." He holds my gaze. "I love you, Rosie. I don't know why such a smart, beautiful, funny, kind, and sexy as hell girl wants me, but I'm not going to look a gift horse in the mouth."

"You don't get it, do you? You get back what you give out. I get that now. It's taken a long time for it to sink in for me, but I get it. You have this reputation; everyone thinks you're this bad boy, but I've only ever seen the good in you. You are a good person, but for some reason, you didn't believe it."

"I do now. You've made me see that I have good in me, that I have talent, even brains and that I can be a good guy. I guess you bring out the best in me."

"Ditto. I would never have thought that I would have the confidence, courage, and self-belief to do what I've done since I met you. My mum might change now that I've had things out with her. She might not, but I believe in myself now; that's all that matters. And, you have more than helped with that."

"We're gonna be so good together, Rosie. You and me."

I pull my arms a little tighter around his neck. "Yeah. We are. We're going to be the strongest non-fake couple around."

We seal the deal with a kiss before heading back inside.

Epiogue

Riley

Two weeks later. The day before Christmas Eve.

"I'm so excited, Rosie. An actual party hosted by us. I don't believe it!" I'm so excited and happy to have my friend back. I can't believe I nearly lost her over a boy. I'll never let a boy dictate my friendships ever again. Although, it all worked out in the end.

Rosie shakes her head in disbelief. "I don't quite believe it either. This time last Christmas, I was so miserable. Now, I have these amazing friends, the best boyfriend, and I'm having an actual house party."

I roll my eyes. "Alright. We get it. Your life is wonderful. Now, come on. You need to help me look gorgeous; everyone will be here in 10 minutes."

Now, it's her turn to roll her eyes. "Yeah. Like you need any help with that."

"Well, *you* tell me I'm gorgeous all the time. Why don't guys think so?" It doesn't matter what she says. The truth is that guys just don't seem to like me in that way. I must be sending out the wrong signals or something, because no guy ever approaches me.

"Riley, do you not think it might just be because you're intimidating to boys? Your red, curly hair and green eyes just make you stunning. Then, you have this figure to die for; you're always training, so guys know you are so fit that you can run rings around them. And then, there's the small fact that you would have very little time to spend time with a boy. You are always training, and you're right to spend so much time training. I've seen you perform a few times now; I know how good you are. Stick with it, and you will be in the Olympic squad. So, it's just a matter of time. There will be plenty of time for guys."

I shake my head. "Easy for you to say when you have one. No. I know you're right. I don't have time for a guy, but I just wish I'd get the option, you know?"

My stomach flips as Russ walks into the living room and looks at us both. He's the chaperone for the party tonight. I mean, is it wise having a 19-year-old as a chaperone for a teenage party? In normal circumstances, I'd say probably not, but Russ is so serious all the time. He's probably more responsible than her parents.

He looks at Rosie. "You look nice. All dressed up. Don't think I've ever seen you in a dress before." He leans in and kisses her on the cheek. Then, he looks up at me and looks uncomfortable, like he doesn't know whether to kiss me on the cheek or not.

"Hey, Russ," I say quietly.

He clears his throat, and then, his eyes run down my body, taking in my outfit. I decided to go girlie tonight, too. It is Christmas, after all; I don't get many chances to wear dresses. I went for a deep green, body con dress with lace at the top. I don't need a bra. My boobs aren't big enough, and I might as well wear something fitted, might as well show off my slim figure. Lord knows I put enough hours in at the gym. So, I feel nice, sexy even. I'm determined to get guys to notice me. I feel like Russ is looking at me like *he's* noticing me. Yeah, he's too old for me, I know, but still. He is so hot. And, he's always been so lovely to me. Still, I'm 15, and he's 19. So, I can't even see him like that, but he's certainly nice to look at.

"You look beautiful, Riley." Wow. I'm taken aback. No one has ever said I look beautiful before. Early Christmas present for me.

I smile at him. "Thanks. Happy birthday for yesterday. Nineteen . . . Wow."

He smiles at me, and my insides do a flippy thing. "Yeah. Thanks. When do you turn 16?"

"January . . . Not long now."

He looks thoughtful. "Cool . . . Well, enjoy the party. You get any trouble, you come to me, yeah?"

I frown. "Why would I get trouble?"

He looks me up and down again. It's quick, but I catch it. "You look . . . The way you look tonight... Just, you may get a lot of attention. Just come to me if any of it is unwanted."

"Wow. Thanks. I will. I doubt I will need you, but thanks for the offer."

"I wouldn't be too sure about that," he mutters as he wonders off.

Liam walks in as I watch Russ leave. He knocks on the open door of the living room. He's a regular face at Rosie's now. His family don't mind him spending so much time here. Liam's home life isn't up to much, according to the little bits that Rosie has told me. She hasn't gone into detail, but his parents work a lot. So, Rosie's mum and dad are happy for him to hang out here as long as they're not here alone. If they go to her bedroom, the door has to be open at all times.

"Hello. We all ready?"

Rosie turns around and grins at him. "Liam!"

She always looks so happy to see him. I wish I had what they had. I'm over my crush now. When you see your crush looking at your best friend like she hung the moon, you tend to get over it.

He goes over to her. "You look so beautiful," I hear him say to her in a quiet voice. He leans in to kiss her.

"No! You can't kiss me; I've just done my lipstick," she squeals.

"Tough," he says. "Do it again in a minute."

He kisses her without any argument from Rosie. They're so happy. They couldn't be more opposite. She's brainy and quiet, and he's the bad boy of the school. Or, he was. Rosie is a good influence. They might be different, but the truth is that they are a perfect match.

I make myself scarce and go downstairs to see if Russ needs any help. He has his back to me in the kitchen. He's so tall now, and I notice how broad his shoulders are. Nice.

"Hey. You need any help?"

He spins around, startled. "Hey. I didn't hear you come down."

I laugh. "Sorry."

He looks at my mouth. "Where's Rosie?"

"She's upstairs."

He nods, walks toward me, and puts his hand on my shoulder, brushing my hair down my back. "Don't settle, Riley. You won't settle, will you?" His voice sounds gravelly.

"What do you mean?"

"I heard you saying that boys don't pay any attention to you, that you want to get their attention. You deserve a guy who knows what he has when he has you. You won't settle for anything less, right?"

Okay. What is happening here? "Of course not. I won't."

"Promise?"

I nod. "I promise."

"Good." He pats me on the arm as though I'm a child, needing to be comforted. Okay. What was that about?

129

"Wait." He looks startled. "Who is Rosie with?"

"Liam. Why?"

His eyes widen, and he runs to the bottom of the stairs. "Liam, Rosie, get down here. Now! No being alone in the bedroom tonight while I'm on duty."

I laugh. "You don't have to worry about those two, you know."

Rosie and Liam make their way downstairs. "Russ, behave. What do you think we will do up there?"

"I don't want to know. Just no disappearing, okay? I'm in charge tonight."

She pats his arm. "Ah, always so sensible, following the rules, doing the right thing, aren't you big brother?"

She walks past him. I look up at him. His eyes are on me again, something unfathomable in them. "Yeah. I guess."

They both walk up to me, hand in hand. "Come on, Riles. Let's find you the man of your dreams."

I look over my shoulder, and Russ is watching me walk away.

Interesting.

The End

Arrowsmith High Book Two: Russ and Riley's Story is now available! Click to get Meet Me at the Gym delivered to your Kindle and it is also available on KU.

Chapter One below;

Prologue – Meet Me at the Gym

Riley

How bad would it be, really, if I fell flat on my face? Yeah. Bad. That can't happen. I can do this. I've practised this routine so many times that I could do it in my sleep. The line of judges watching and hundreds of people in the audience don't make my butterflies any better, but I've got this.

I bite my lip and smooth down my purple leotard with sweaty hands; purple is the new team colour. I try to put to the back of my mind how it clashes with my red, curly hair. I'm sure the last thing the judges will care about is if my skin tone goes with my outfit. There is one thing and one thing only that they're interested in: gymnastics and how precise I can be with my moves.

I close my eyes and inhale slowly as the music starts. As soon as I take that first step onto the mat, that's it; all the nerves disappear. How I do today and what everyone expects of me, everyone pinning their hopes on me, vanishes, and it's just me and the music and the mat, my comfort zone, my happy place. It shows.

My opener is so good that I know I will sail into the rest of the routine if I get it right. I start to run, picking up speed as I go, and then take the leap, a forward somersault and a twist then turn around into a backflip and spring. I nail it! My heart soars as I continue with the rest of the routine. It's over in minutes. This is going to be a good score; I know it. I turn to the crowd with my finishing backflip into a twisting somersault and land smoothly, get my balance, and my arms go up into the air. I give a slow smile and let out a huge breath. I did it. I see big smiles from my coach, and all my teammates are whooping and clapping as I make my way back to them, my face flushed.

If I could bottle this feeling right now, the exhilaration, the high I get from doing this, I would be the richest girl on the planet because there is nothing like it.

Winning at life is what it feels like, even if it is for 10 minutes while everyone is watching. Winning. It's something that is ridiculously important to me.

As I reach them, Coach Marie comes over and pats me on the shoulder. "Bloody amazing as always! You always deliver, Riley, and that twist backflip was perfection. You've got this comp in the bag."

I grin widely. She's my mentor, my coach, *sometimes* my friend, but sometimes my worst enemy. She pushes me to my limit, but I have immense respect for her.

She hugs me, and I exhale; I've made her proud. I look into the crowd to find the other person I want to make proud, my dad. I search the crowd, and my eyes land on a beautiful, brown, familiar pair of eyes staring straight at me. My stomach lurches as my heartbeat quickens even more. My mouth goes dry. *What is Russ doing here?* He watched me. Next to him, my best friend, Rosie, is smiling broadly at me and waving rapidly. Rosie has been saying that she wants to come and watch me. I love that she bought a ticket to this event, but why did she bring her brother? And why do I react like this every time I see him? I turn into a bumbling idiot. I can't even get my words out. On a quick glance, I see he is looking as good as always, his brown hair just long enough that it comes down onto his forehead. He is head and shoulders above Rosie... And what shoulders they are, broad from all the sports he does; he's in good shape. All that aside, there is something about him that I can't put my finger on, an intenseness there that I recognise in myself.

Get a grip, Riley.

He's 19. Three years difference might not seem like a lot when you're in your 30s or whatever, but a just-turned 16-year-old girl and a 19-year-old boy wouldn't go down too well right now. He sees me as his kid sisters' friend, someone who is way too young for him. The way he looks at me sometimes, though... It's as though he sees me. Still, as much as I shouldn't let my head go there, I can't help but appreciate everything that is Russ because there is so much to appreciate. He is lush in every way, and the slight smile on his face right now might be small yet so beautiful.

I shake my head to bring myself back into the now. Dad is sitting next to Rosie, cheering and clapping, and my heart warms at the sight of him, never missing a competition unless work doesn't allow it. He's my number one supporter. After Mum left, he could have crumbled, but he didn't. He stepped up and is a better parent than she could ever have been, and for that, I'm so, so grateful. I wave at them all. I'm not allowed to go to them just yet, not until the competition finishes. I take a seat with the rest of my club as they all congratulate me on my floor performance, my peers patting me on the back, the little ones looking at me in awe. I remember all too well being the little one, looking at the big ones with the same look they're giving me right now. I take a deep breath and smile to myself; I'm doing ok. I still have my beam to do, and I've already done the bars. I just hope that knowing Russ is in the audience now won't make my nerves take over my performance, because the thought of him watching me is making me want to be sick.

****

I step down from the podium, giving Dad and the rest of them a big grin and a thumbs-up, heat radiating from my chest with my first place medal dangling from my neck. I'm so happy. In fact, happy doesn't even cover it. I've made everyone proud, my dad, my club, Rosie... And Russ. I wonder what he thought, if he was impressed. Rosie says he's grumpy all the time at home. He's never like that when I've seen him, but Rosie says he's different with me than he is with everyone else. She thinks he has a soft spot for me; he doesn't. He's just nicer to me than his little sister, and that's not hard. He has a girlfriend anyway. She's new, but I hate how jealous I am about it. Rosie said she's pretty and seems nice. That makes it worse.

Everyone is waiting for me once the ceremony is over, and I go up to them.

Dad is holding his arms open. "Honey, you were fantastic! I knew as soon as you finished your floor routine that, unless something went totally wrong on the beam, that first spot was yours. Everyone in the audience went crazy. It was breathtaking."

"Thanks, Dad," I say, prying myself away from his hug.

Rosie speaks. "Oh, my God! I never knew... I mean, I knew you did a lot of training and won medals and stuff, but I didn't know you were *that* good. You should be on TV. You are 100 percent going to the Olympics. How did I not know that my best friend could do that?"

I roll my eyes. "Shut up." The flush creeps up my cheeks. Russ is standing to the side of her, and my ears are getting hot with embarrassment. I am purposely not looking at him.

"Seriously, I am in awe. You deserve first place. I'm a big fat lump of mud or something stood here with you right now after seeing what you can do and how you can throw yourself around!"

I laugh. "Rosie, seriously. Shut up."

"No, she's right." I hear Russ's deep voice.

Rosie's head snaps around to look at him, a scowl on her face.

Russ shakes his head. "Not about you, sis. About her." He turns to look at me. "Seriously good, Riles. Seriously." He's a man of few words, but he gets the point across fine. I try not to feel all warm and gushy inside at his words. I fail. I can't help it; he gets to me, and it's about time I just accept it.

"Thanks," I say quietly, unable to make eye contact with him. I'm usually not quiet or shy, but for some reason, I am around him. I hate it, hate that I have that reaction to him.

"Hey," he says so that I'll look at him.

I do what he wants and look at him.

"You're welcome." He winks at me.

He winks! My lips part as I draw in a breath. *He just winked at me.*

I look at Rosie. I need to be normal and quick; she is frowning at me. "You ok, Riley?" she asks.

I nod, my eyes quickly flitting to Russ and then back to her. "Sure. Just excited, you know, for the next stage."

She grins. "When is your next competition?"

"I've got the nationals in a month, and there is a competition for Europe that takes place in Madrid."

"Yup. She's a busy girl, my girl," Dad says.

He's right. It's going to involve a lot of training and hard work, but if I continue on this route, I will make it to the Olympics as long as I don't let things get in my way, things like parties and boys... And crushes on my best friend's brother. Things like that.

How easy it would be to let him distract me. Those brown eyes, with eyelashes... They should be illegal. Yes, I've examined them and those lips. When they smile at me, those lips make me feel like I'm the only girl that exists.

I look around at everyone greeting their families, everyone being congratulated. The atmosphere of the gym never fails to get to me. I remember how it just felt up there on that podium. Being there, receiving a gold medal at the Olympics, would be a million times better. I have to do it, not just for Dad or for Coach but for me. It's what I want. But getting what I want brings consequences, and those consequences are no time for boys or for socialising. I look back at my dad; he's looking at me with such admiration, so proud. Nope. That's it. I will not get distracted, and I *will* do this. I want that Olympic gold medal, and nothing is going to stop me, even if it means sacrifices.

Chapter 1

Riley

I stare out of the bus window while I wait for Rosie, not really taking in the view. Instead, I'm going through my new routine in my head. I see her and Liam walk towards the bus and smile. They are so cute together, and who knew Liam had a soft side? I'm still sad that my crush fell for my best friend, but what can I do about it? One way to get over your crush is to have your best friend fall for him; it really helps you get over him super quickly. Besides, that's all it was, just a crush.

I'm the queen of crushes. I seem to get a new one every couple of months. I'm not stupid enough to think that real feelings were involved. Liam had never even spoken to me before Rosie came to our school and started hanging out with me. Rosie and I couldn't look more different. She's a curvy brunette, and I'm a skinny redhead. Liam is gorgeous, though. No doubt about it, but he only has eyes for Rosie. That's fine by me.

She steps on the bus, and her eyes fall on me. She sits beside me, and Liam sits in the empty seat adjacent. The minibus that takes us to and from school is practically full now; all the regular faces are here.

"Hey, babe. How was food tech?" Rosie asks me.

I shrug. "I produced the best crumble ever made."

Rosie rolls her eyes. "Competitive much?"

I laugh. *Yup. Self-confessed.*

Liam shouts, "Mine would have been the best, you know, if I'd remembered the ingredients."

I huff as Rosie's head spins to where he's sat. "What? Why didn't you take the ingredients? Did you get into trouble?"

He winks at her. "Doesn't matter, does it? I'm not gonna be making apple crumble in the future."

"Argh." She turns to me, frowning. "He makes me so mad. I hate it that he doesn't just stick to the rules."

"Babe, you love it when I don't stick to the rules," he says, smirking.

She shakes her head at me. "I don't. I really don't."

My best friend is a stickler for the rules. How she found herself dating the guy that likes breaking them all is beyond me.

Liam looks over at me. "Heard how awesome you were yesterday. Well done and all that."

I blush, not used to his attention. "Thanks."

Rosie smiles at me. "You were awesome."

Liam leans back into his seat. "Yeah. Russ was saying that you were head and shoulders above the rest."

I straighten in my seat and raise my eyebrows. *Russ was talking about me?* "Russ said that?"

Rosie tilts her head at me, assessing my reaction. I may have mentioned to her in the past that her brother is hot. I know he's her brother, but she has eyes; she can see how good looking he is, but if I don't tone down my reactions when he's mentioned, she will twig that I'm crushing on him bad.

Liam is oblivious. "Yeah. He said you've seriously got moves, and you are the fittest girl he's ever seen."

My eyes widen, and my breath catches in my throat. *He said I was fit?* "He said that?"

"Yeah. Said that based on the speed you go at to enable you to make the moves you can, you must train four hours a day or something. He said your fitness levels are off the charts."

Okay. So, any hope that was building in me comes crashing down and dissipates. He meant physical fitness levels. Of course, he did.

"Oh, yeah." I try to keep the disappointment out of my voice.

He turns to Rosie. "Is he still seeing that girl? What's she called? Carrie?"

I lean in more intently. I am way too interested in anything that involves Russ.

Rosie shakes her head. "I think so. He seems to like her; she's okay, I guess. She doesn't make much of an effort to talk to me, but I've only met her a couple of times. Maybe she's shy."

I shrug. "I haven't met her."

"You coming over later?" Rosie asks me.

Monday is my night off from the gym. I usually go and hang. "Yeah. If that's okay."

Liam shouts over my answer, "What about me?"

Rosie rolls her eyes. "You have friends, babe. You'll manage."

I chuckle to myself. It's so good to see how relaxed she is with him. It's a different Rosie than the one that started at our school in September.

"I'm gonna run over, get my exercise in for the day."

She shakes her head. " No way. It's dark by then."

"I go running all the time, in the morning and at night, and it's dark. It's fine. I can outrun anyone anyway."

"Are you sure?"

I nod. "Of course. My dad will come for me when I'm ready to go home."

I have been running for as long as I can remember, and I live in a neighbourhood where nothing ever happens. I'm not scared to be out alone.

Running is a favourite pastime of mine. I love to just be able to forget everything else and focus on my feet hitting the pavement. Fitness and keeping in good shape are my mindfulness. It keeps me in a good place.

****

It's a crisp, clear night as I set out on my run. I check my Fitbit to see how many steps I work up on my run. I lose myself in the rhythm of my footsteps and my music. I have my running playlist on and am in my happy zone, dressed in gym leggings and a long-sleeved t-shirt with a fleece over top; it's a cold February night even though I'll be working up a sweat.

I'm five minutes away from Rosie's house when I see them on the road ahead. It's not something I would normally bother about, approaching a group of boys, but it's particularly deserted on the streets tonight. I can see their heads turn my way. Maybe it's just a coincidence that they're looking in my direction. I've never seen them before. I reach to my arm where my phone is in an armband and turn the music off, but I leave my earphones in. They're laughing, and their eyes are definitely still on me. I exhale as I run with trepidation towards them. There are four of them. It's dark, and they're in hoodies, apart from one of them in a bright red puffa jacket. They all get in a line, shoulder to shoulder, as I approach, and my stomach plummets. They're going to stop me from getting past. I know this area; there is nowhere I can detour. I slow down to a leisurely jog. Maybe I could pretend I'm going to a house. I glance up the lane. There are no houses immediately near me; they're way up the road. *No! Why is it so quiet tonight?* There are no cars in sight. I glance across the road and decide to cross quickly. I have my earphones in, so I quickly reach up and pull them out, grabbing for my phone to call Dad.

"Hey! Where are you running off to?"

My stomach plummets. Images start flashing through my mind. They could attack me here, and no one would know until Rosie realises I'm late. I put my head down and keep running, ignoring them.

I hear another one of them shout, "Hey! We're talking to you."

I still say nothing and carry on, going faster. Just as I start to get my hopes up that I'm going to get past them, two other guys step out of an alley in front of me and block my path.

"Where are you going? My friends want to speak to you. Don't be rude."

I have no choice but to come to a stop. My mouth goes dry. I look around. The other four have joined us now. I'm surrounded by six boys.

"Do you want something?" My voice is shaking as I try to sound normal.

One of them beside me nods. "Yeah. We want to have a chat. We're bored. You look like you'd be fun. Stay and talk to us."

"I'm sorry, but I have somewhere I have to be." *Is that my voice? Don't show them you're scared, Riley. They will feed off it.*

"What are you doing out here on your own? It's like you're asking for trouble," the guy in the red coat says to me in a low, steady voice. He stares at me, waiting for an answer and cold chills run up and down my body. He is creepy. Dangerous.

Think, Riley.

I take a deep breath. If I'm nice to them, maybe they'll relax, and I can somehow get past them. I try to make my voice sound as normal as possible. "I am going to my friend's. I thought I would run there. She's expecting me, actually, so I need to go."

"In a minute," one of them says. "You look in good shape. I guess you must run around here a lot."

Not anymore, I won't. "Not really."

This situation just got serious. I don't know any of these guys; they don't go to my school. If they're still even in school.

Think, Riley.

Keeping my calm is the main thing. My dad has always said that if you get yourself in a situation you can't handle, always believe you can handle it, and the way forward will be clear. They don't know me or what I'm capable of. They have no idea how strong I am. My upper body is strong enough to do the bars. I can barge past these guys if they're not expecting it, right? I'm only five minutes away from Rosie's. If I go at full speed, I'll be faster than all of them, but I need to move quickly.

The one that is scaring me, the one in the red coat, grabs my arm roughly. "You're not going anywhere until we tell you that you can leave."

One of the other guys speaks. "Dude, let her go. You're hurting her."

The red coat guy doesn't say anything. He just stares at me, giving me the chills. His grip on my arm is painful.

"Come on. Hang with us a while."

Bile rises in my throat. I will not let my mind go to a dark place. I'm getting past these guys. I wiggle my arm free, and he drops his hand. A car comes into view, thank God! As it comes, they all step back a little, probably so they won't look suspicious. As the car comes to pass, I realise that they're not going to know anything is wrong, and they're not going to stop. *Crap!* Still, it *is* distracting the boys. Now is my chance.

I muster everything I have and barge quickly through the two stood in front of me. I manage it and take off running.

"Hey! We're not done talking with you yet!"

They start to chase me, but they can't match my speed. No way. I run as fast as I can. Instead of going my usual route to Rosie's, I make my way to the main road where there should be more traffic; safety in numbers. I strain my ears to see if I can hear them behind me, but all I can hear is my rapid breathing and my footsteps. I turn to see if they're behind me but lose my footing. The trouble is, going at the speed I'm going, I go flying into the air, my head hitting the pavement. The momentum of my fall carries me forward, and my head scrapes across the pavement. I yelp in pain and am momentarily dazed. I shake my head to right myself. I need to get up and quick before they catch me. I force myself back onto my feet and carry on running. I hope to God they're not coming in my direction now because my speed has slowed considerably. I can see Rosie's house and nearly cry. My legs are going to give way. Something warm and wet from my forehead trickles down, contrasting against the cold winter air. I need to get there fast. My adrenaline is running out by the second.

If you want to keep up to date on any coming releases, beta reader offers, or other things, then please sign up to my newsletter.

Thank you so much for reading my novel. I hope you enjoyed it! The best way to thank an author for writing a great book is to leave an honest review. I would be so grateful if you did that.

About Author

I'm a Northern girl born and bred, living in a little town near Manchester, England, where I like to do fun stuff with my kids, spending time with friends, and watching American TV shows with my husband.

I discovered my love for reading at a very early age by reading Charlotte's Web, then onto Sweet Valley High series, in my teens, my mum introduced me to Mills & Boon and I've been a goner for a good romance ever since.

I've recently had a break from writing, due to caring for my parents and working as a childminder, but I missed writing so much I have somehow managed to fit it back into my schedule.

I was a legal assistant for many years before I started a family. Now I am a personal slave and taxi to my two young children and wouldn't have it any other way.

Printed in Great Britain
by Amazon

87268626R00081